150901/20-
453 9/15

BCL

D0847789

THE FIELD
Book of
COUNTRY HOUSES
AND THEIR OWNERS

THE FIELD
Book of
COUNTRY HOUSES
AND THEIR OWNERS
Family Seats of the British Isles

HUGH MONTGOMERY-MASSINGBERD

Webb & Bower

MICHAEL JOSEPH

DEDICATED TO JAMES LEES-MILNE

First published in Great Britain 1988 by
Webb & Bower (Publishers) Limited
9 Colleton Crescent, Exeter, Devon EX2 4BY
in association with Michael Joseph Limited
27 Wright's Lane, London W8 5TZ

Designed by Ron Pickless

Production by Nick Facer/Rob Kendrew

Text this edition © 1988 Hugh Montgomery-Massingberd
Illustrations this edition © 1988 The Field Magazine

British Library Cataloguing in Publication Data

Montgomery-Massingberd, Hugh, 1946–
The Field book of country houses and their owners:
family seats of the British Isles.
1. Great Britain. Country houses
I. Title
941

ISBN 0-86350-234-2

All rights reserved. No part of this publication
may be reproduced, stored in a retrieval system, or
transmitted, in any form or by any means, electronic,
mechanical, photocopying, recording or otherwise,
without the prior permission of the copyright holder.

Phototypeset in Great Britain by Keyspools Limited, Golborne,
Lancashire

Colour reproduction by Peninsular Repro Service Limited,
Exeter, Devon

Printed and bound in Italy by New Interlitho SPA, Milan

CONTENTS

INTRODUCTION

In an old Mae West film the siren enters a night-club swathed in furs and rocks. As Miss West gives up her coat, the hat-check girl exclaims: 'Goodness! What diamonds'. Mae drawls back: '*Goodness* had nothing to do with it'.

Similarly when people witter on, as they do *ad nauseam*, about the 'national heritage', it should be stressed that the *nation* had nothing to do with it. For what is called the 'heritage' of country houses was, of course, created by families who through their foresight and good stewardship have preserved the very fabric of the countryside.

A hundred years ago there were some 10,000 'family seats' in the British Isles—that is to say country houses, from castles to manor houses, in traditional private occupation and supported by agricultural estates, great and small. Today—after a series of acute agricultural depressions, a couple of World Wars and the relentless onslaught of confiscatory capital taxation—there are barely 2,000.

Despite the booming 'heritage industry' and the recent growth of the cult of the country house, the majority of these surviving seats are almost completely unknown. While the grossly over-exposed 'statelies' are 'revisited' over and over again, their poor relations, the hidden halls and minor houses, too often remain unrecorded—though they are every bit as important to the true heritage as their grander neighbours.

Over the dozen years I contributed regularly to *The Field* (1976–1987), my prime concern was to celebrate and record the privately owned heritage. What particularly disturbed me was that so many long-established families were being parted from their 'illustrious obscure' country houses; they were going largely unmourned and unnoticed—seldom, if ever, to be replaced by a potential new squirearchical dynasty.

It seemed worthwhile to record something of what was left, to celebrate the survival of some lesser-known country houses still in private hands. The idea was to reveal not only the architectural history of the buildings but to set the houses in their proper social and economic context with details of the property's devolution and the present management of the estate.

I compiled a list of houses that had been owned by a family for at least a generation or so and that had not already been written about elsewhere (or in other words in *Country Life* which rather seemed to have lost interest in the dimmer sort of seat) and devised a scheme for their coverage. When I first offered my concept to *The Field*, which I had always thought of as the squires' paper, at the end of the 1970s, the then editor demurred. Happily in 1984 the new editor, Simon Courtauld, lately deputy editor of *The Spectator*, encouraged me to put my 'Family Seats' proposal into practice.

And so, for the three and a half years of the Courtauld editorship I went on a journey of discovery around the British Isles, recording little known seats from Banffshire to Brecon, County Roscommon to Huntingdonshire (none of these wretched 'new counties' for me). From the start, I focused attention on the owners struggling to maintain their beloved homes, seeking to present a relaxed, idiosyncratic and anecdotal portrait sympathetic to the particular flavour and atmosphere of each highly individual family seat.

Looking back now on the places I wrote about, I would tend to categorize them not so much according to architectural style of the building (most are an accumulation of different periods) as to the varying times for which they have been held as the seats of their particular family. Thus, in this abridged selection of about a third of the total covered, I have arranged them in a loose chronological sequence.

PART I

THE MIDDLE AGES

CRUWYS OF CRUWYS MORCHARD

Mr and Mrs Guy Cruwys with their youngest child, Belinda.

THE large county of Devon is remarkably well stocked with un-pretentious seats which remain, against considerable odds, the homes of long-established squires. On the whole these families have been quiet and stay-at-home, with few titles or famous names in their pedigrees, their low profile through the centuries doubtless having much to do with their survival.

Titles or fame, however, surely count for little beside the proud distinction of being, say, Fulford of Fulford, Fursdon of Fursdon, Kelly of Kelly or Spurway of Spurway—to name four Devon familes descended from a medieval ancester who took his surname from lands which they still hold. Another example is Cruwys of Cruwys Morchard, though the well-wooded estate near Tiverton passed through the female line in the early 19th century.

In Prince's *Devon Worthies* (1699) the old saw is quoted: 'Crocker, Cruwys, and Coplestone, When the Conqueror came, were at Home'. Unfortunately, this jolly image of Squire Cruwys (pronounced more or less as in 'Cruise' and deriving from 'Cross') being seated at Cruwys Morchard in 1066 is not borne out by the facts.

Opposite
Cruwys Morchard House, Devon: entrance front.

Cruwys Morchard: the hall in the early 1900s.

The pedigree pieced together from the impressive collection of medieval documents preserved at Cruwys Morchard begins at the end of the 12th century. Robert de Cruwys is mentioned in a pipe roll (one of the annual accounts rendered to the Exchequer by the sheriff of the county) of 1175.

The first of the family to be knighted seems to have been Sir Alexander Cruwys, mentioned in an assize roll for 1238 concerning a dispute over cattle. From *Devon Worthies* we learn that in 1323 the Cruwys Morchard estate

came to be much Impaired by the Heat and Violence of Sir *Alex. Cruwys*, Kt. who in the days of K.E.3 unhappily quarelling with Carew on *Bicklegh Bridg*, ran him thorow and the Rails breaking, threw him in to the

River. Whose pardon ... cost him two and twenty Mannors of Land. Notwithstanding which, there remained a noble Estate to the Heir.

The heir, Robert, appears to have more than lived up to the nobility of his estate, distinguishing himself in the Battle of Crécy in 1346. His return from the wars, 'loaden with Trophies of Honour' (including a knightood), must have been a great day for Cruwys Morchard.

The next Cruwys to venture forth from Cruwys Morchard, Thomas, met with rather less luck than his great-grandfather. A Lancastrian supporter in the Wars of the Roses, Thomas Cruwys was on the losing side at the decisive Battle of Towton in Yorkshire in 1461. Although he received a royal pardon from the victorious Edward IV (still preserved at Cruwys Morchard), Thomas was obliged to forfeit a large amount of land.

Ten years later Thomas loyally trooped off with the other Devonian followers of the Red Rose to greet Queen Margaret (Henry VI's wife) at Weymouth. Within a week of another crushing defeat for the Lancastrians at Tewkesbury, Thomas was dead—either of wounds or the executioner's axe.

Having backed the wrong horse (and mare) in one domestic conflict, the Cruwys family were more prudent a couple of centuries later in the Civil War. Henry Cruwys, whose father had sold off a significant part of the estate in the 1630s, is said to have had Parliamentary leanings; indeed, at the Restoration it was stated that he had been a Captain of Dragoons in the Parliamentary Army and that some-one had seen him 'severall tymes lead & march his company'.

Nonetheless, when John Penruddock's Royalist men marched on Tiverton in 1655 and the mayor of the town sent a message to Henry Cruwys to bring his 'trayned bands' to help in its defence, the squire replied to the messenger 'that he would not doe itt neither would he stir a foote out of house for the matter'.

Although Henry's son actually married a Foote (heiress of the local MP), this riposte nicely summed up the philosophy of a squirearchical dynasty set upon sur-vival. Since the 18th century, the Lords of the Manor of Cruwys Morchard have tended to combine administration of their ancestral acres with careers in the law and the church. Thus, Samuel Cruwys, a Fellow of the Royal Society, became Re-corder of South Molton in 1744; his son, John, was the bachelor 'squarson' of Cruwys Morchard.

At the time of Squarson John, Cruwys Morchard House had 'pallisades in front of the house and the entrance was in the middle'. The history of the house is not so well documented as the family pedigree. The present building, clearly a Georgian remodelling, seems to be on the site of the original manor house.

There are various features providing evidence of the earlier house such as the hammerbeam roof in the old kitchen and a datestone of 1594. The wing to the right of the seven-bay entrance facade, containing the library, dates from 1682. Inside, the drawing-room has a pretty frieze and a handsome fireplace—though the house is surprisingly short of 17th- or 18th-century chimney-pieces.

Squarson John's cousin and successor, the Reverend Henry Shortrudge Cruwys, clearly found his inheritance hard going at the end of the 18th century. He wrote that:

> . . . the house is so damp that I am obliged in the winter to shift from parlour to parlour, and to the Library to prevent the Heir Looms from rotting. Nay, when I went lately to South Molton, I locked up a room and at my Return, tho' absent only five days, the Furniture was as white as a Barber's shop.

For the first time in more than 600 years the male line descent of Cruwys Mor-chard was broken when the estate passed in 1804 to Squarson Henry's son-in-law, George Sharland, husband of his daugh-ter Harriet. The name of Cruwys was happily revived under Royal Licence in 1831 by the Sharlands' son, another Squarson, the Reverend George Sharland Cruwys.

Squarson George made considerable improvements to the house and estate. It was probably he who added the parapet (an old drawing at Cruwys Morchard shows the house before this addition and also a tithe barn where the present gates now stand) and imported the fine oak staircase from Enmore Castle in Somerset.

The present front door, with its fanlight and Ionic columns, was also brought in from elsewhere only a few years ago by the present squire's son, Guy Cruwys. This pleasing addition came from Bampton House in Tiverton.

Born in 1946 and educated nearby at Blundells and Exeter University, Mr Cruwys practises as a solicitor in Tiverton as well as running the 1,400-acre estate. His father, Edgar Cruwys, a former JP for Devon, now lives in the Isle of Man with his wife Peggy, having secured the future of Cruwys Morchard, reafforested the estate and restored the house.

When Edgar, a squadron-leader in the RAF, inherited the place from a childless uncle, Captain Lewis Cruwys, in 1957, the house did not even have electricity. Lewis and his wife, Margaret, an anti-quary and author of the invaluable *Cruwys Morchard Notebook*, liked to keep things as they were.

Guy Cruwys is married to Sarah Good-son from another well-known Devon family and they have one son and three daughters. It is delightful to report that Cruwys Morchard, in the countryside near Exmoor, basks in the cheerful atmos-phere of its eponymous family.

Cruwys Morchard House, Pennymoor, near Tiverton, Devon, is not open to the public, though public events are occasionally held on the estate.

DYMOKE OF SCRIVELSBY

The lion-guarded gate of Scrivelsby Court, Lincolnshire.

'THE Honourable the Queen's Champion and Standard Bearer of England' is the sort of impressive handle one might expect to come across among the credits of a duke, but in fact this hereditary office is held by an untitled squire from that least known of counties, Lincolnshire—Lieutenant-Colonel John Lindley Marmion Dymoke.

Kitted out in the late-Victorian full dress uniform of the Royal Lincolnshire Regiment, the then Captain Dymoke carried the Union Standard in Westminster Abbey at the present Queen's Coronation in 1953. Today the Champion runs the 3,000-acre family estate at Scrivelsby on the edge of the still undiscovered Lincolnshire Wolds—land which has not been bought or sold since the Norman Conquest.

Champions were, in effect, medieval 'minders' (shades of Dennis Waterman). As with many traditions, the origins of the office are obscure and by the time the colourful ceremony of throwing down the gauntlet became part of the English coronation ritual it was essentially a poetic fiction. There is no documentary evidence that it was performed before the coronation of Richard II in 1377 when Sir John Dymoke did the honours.

This knight, supposedly from Dymock in Gloucestershire, had established his claim to be King's Champion in the right of his wife, Margaret, the owner of the Scrivelsby estate and coheiress of the Marmions, traditionally Champions to the Dukes of Normandy in pre-Conquest days. The Manor of Scrivelsby has descended with the Championship.

Despite the occasional curious counter-claim from romantically-minded kinsmen (such as, for instance, the novelist Anthony Powell's great-grandfather, Dymoke Welles), the Dymokes have turned up at coronations in their ceremonial role ever since. 'There is no record of anybody having taken up the challenge,' the present Champion says. 'Not surprising, since the ceremony was per-

Above
Scrivelsby: entrance front.

formed before a very much invited audience.'

The secret of survival for the squire-archy, on the whole, has been to keep a low profile over the centuries, but being hereditary Champions to the sovereign has inevitably drawn the Dymokes of Scrivelsby into the occasional tight corner. Sir Thomas Dymoke, who acted as Champion at Edward IV's coronation in 1461, ended on the block on the orders of his erratic royal master after being implicated in the 'Kingmaker's Plot' to restore Henry VI during the Wars of the Roses.

Royal favour was restored to Sir Thomas's son, Sir Robert Dymoke, who was Henry VIII's treasurer of Tournay; though Sir Robert's own son, Edward, had an unenviable stint as Sheriff of Lincolnshire in 1536 during insurrection in the county which formed part of the 'Pilgrimage of Grace' risings against the Dissolution of the Monasteries.

In the 17th century the Dymokes, like so may loyal squires, suffered near financial ruin in the Civil War. The Champion to Charles I was splendidly generous, in life and death, to the royal cause, and his cousin had to pay an enormous fine to the Cromwellians for bearing this 'lewd and malicious title'.

The ceremony at the coronation ban-

The Champion's gauntlet used at George III's Coronation, 1761.

quet in Westminster Hall did not always proceed without mishap. After James II's Champion, Sir Charles Dymoke, had issued the challenge and dismounted, he was advancing to kiss the sovereign's hand when 'he fell down all his length in the hall'. At George III's coronation the steed of the Lord High Steward escorting the Champion literally reversed his training procedure by backing into the Hall and, amid much merriment, proceeded to present its rump to the bemused monarch.

The next coronation, that of George IV, was the occasion for a highly spectacular display of early-19th-century romantic medievalism when Henry Dymoke—son of the then Dymoke of Scrivelsby who was in Holy Orders—rode up gorgeously attired on a horse supplied by Astley's Circus and threw down the gauntlet. It was the last time the ceremony was performed.

While the hoots of laughter were echoing in the ears of George III's Champion at the 1761 coronation, the Tudor Scrivelsby Court was being burnt down. Its successor, a Gothic pile, fell into disrepair in the later years of the present squire's eccentric grandfather who died in 1946. Frank Dymoke, who carried the Standard of England at the coronation of Edward VII, George V and George VI, ended up as a solitary recluse on the first floor of Scrivelsby Court.

The story goes that his only link with the outside world was a basket which he lowered from a window for messages or sustenance. During an unsuccessful attempt to visit the Champion in 1943, James Lees-Milne saw 'an ashen face with a snow white beard, completely expressionless, pressed against the glass pane' of an upper window.

After the old squire's death the Scrivelsby estate (and thus the Championship) passed directly to John Dymoke from his grandfather, bypassing his father, 'to alleviate the heavy burden of death duties'. Colonel Dymoke saw little of his grandfather and, out of respectful family piety, remains reluctant to add further anecdotes to the local folklore concerning his odd predecessor.

There is certainly nothing strange about the 33rd Lord of the Manor of Scrivelsby who is everything a squire should be—active farmer and public-spirited landlord, Deputy Lieutenant for Lincolnshire and a former High Sheriff, a district councillor and a school governor,

Lieutenant-Colonel and Mrs John Dymoke.

chairman of the county branch of the Country Landowners Association, and so forth. Since retiring from the Army in 1972 (having commanded the Royal Anglian Regiment), Colonel Dymoke has devoted himself to running the estate.

The hopelessly dilapidated Scrivelsby Court was demolished in the 1950s and, at the end of that climacteric decade for the English country house, the Dymokes set about converting the Elizabethan gatehouse of the previous Court (the one destroyed by fire during George III's coronation) into a compact and atmospheric family home. Colonel Dymoke married Susan Fane, from Fulbeck in Lincolnshire, shortly after the coronation, and they have three sons to continue the Championship line: the two elder ones, Francis, a chartered accountant, and Philip, a Captain in the Welsh Guards, are both married (the former with a twin son and daughter); the youngest son, Charles, was born in the newly converted Scrivelsby Court in 1961.

The building work, supervised by the architect J. Stanley Wright and incorporating various features from the previous Courts, was done with the help of an Historic Buildings Council grant.

The discerning visitor to Scrivelsby will note the encouraging signs of a well-run estate: the fine new fencing retaining the herd of deer, the replanted trees and plenty more evidence of that responsible form of conservation carried out in such an undervalued manner by private owners of the so-called 'national heritage'. Assisted by a staff of seven, Colonel Dymoke tends about half the estate himself.

The home farm is a mixture of sheep (800 breeding ewes) and arable. 'I am on parade with my men at 07.30 each morning and work (a great pleasure) stops only when the management requirements are complete—no matter whether it's eight, nine, ten or midnight.' Susan Dymoke has created attractive new gardens behind the old gatehouse which are open every year for charity events.

The family history could so easily have ended 40 years ago when Scrivelsby was in ruins, but thanks to dedication and hard work, a remarkable rescue act has been achieved.

Scrivelsby Court, near Horncastle, Lincolnshire, is open by written appointment.

Staunton of Staunton

Mr and Mrs Edmund Staunton

THE Stauntons of Staunton are indubitably the longest-established squirearchical dynasty in Nottinghamshire and in his prize-winning *Shell Guide to Nottinghamshire* the Reverend Henry Thorold has even suggested that the Stauntons, supposedly at Staunton since 1041, may be the oldest family in England still to inhabit the ancestral estate from which they take their name—though admittedly the descent of the property has gone through the female line for the last 300 years.

The enchanting sleepy village off the Great North Road, with the pub sign appropriately bearing the Staunton Arms, evokes a magical atmosphere of antiquity. In the largely 14th-century St Mary's Church to the east of Staunton Hall there is an inscription to the effect that the Stauntons 'inherited the Estate here from the time of the Saxons'. It goes on to describe how 'Sir Malger Staunton defended Belvoir against William Duke of Normandy called William the Conqueror

and had the strongest fortress ever since called (by his name) Staunton Tower'.

Even the most cautious genealogists have to admit that from at least the early 12th century the Stauntons were closely connected with Belvoir Castle (visible across the Vale to the south of Staunton Hall). In his study of Nottinghamshire families the late Mr Keith Train notes that it may well be that Mauger (or Malger), who held the manor of Walter de Aincourt at the time of *Domesday Book* in 1086, was granted the manor of Staunton because of the feudal duty of 'castleguard'.

This meant that the Stauntons were obliged to defend Belvoir Castle in times of crisis. To this day one of the towers at Belvoir is called the Staunton Tower. The tradition is that the golden key of this Tower is presented by the head of the Staunton family when the sovereign comes to the castle. Similarly a bell rope has to be given to Bottesford Church with a view to rousing the inhabitants of the Vale if Belvoir is under threat. The present squire, Edmund Staunton, has con-

Right
Staunton Hall, Nottinghamshire: staircase and hallway.

Above
Staunton: the south (garden) front.

tinued to observe this practice.

Although there is no direct evidence to connect the Domesday Mauger with one Geoffrey de Staunton, recorded as living there in 1150, the latter did call his son Mauger. There is certainly no shortage of documents to prove the descent of Staunton from Geoffrey onwards. The family

story is told in execrable verse by Robert Cade, as published in Robert Thoroton's *Antiquities of Nottinghamshire* (1677): '... Wilyam died in the year of Christ/One thousand, as I guess/Three hundred fortie adding one/Not one year more or lesse', and worse.

Inside the church there is a series of splendid monuments to Staunton knights and ladies of the 13th and 14th centuries. Some of these were damaged in the Civil War when Staunton was sacked by the Cromwellians.

The then squire, Colonel William Staunton, a leading Cavalier who equipped a Nottinghamshire regiment of 1,200 foot and a troop of horse at his own expense for the King, was away when the Roundheads arrived. His brave wife, a Staffordshire Waring, fortified the manor house with pillows, bolsters and mattresses but eventually had to surrender. The bullet holes in the front door are inscribed '1645'.

The architectural history of the present

Left
Staunton: the Great Hall, modernised in the 18th century.

Staunton: a meeting of the Sealed Knot Society held in 1982.

house goes back to the mid-16th century though there was obviously a medieval building here before. There is a date of '1554' in the Ancaster stone and local rubble walls of the north front, whereas the finely carved coat of arms on the porch is dated '1573' and bears the initials 'R' and 'B'—presumably those of Robert Staunton and his wife, Bridget Barwick. Their son, William, a ward of the 3rd Earl of Rutland, married a Miss Disney— doubtless a kinswoman of Walt's who hailed from an ancient line.

This tradition of wardship by the Rutlands was to land the Stauntons in financial difficulties. The 5th Earl disposed of his wardship of William's son to a Mr

Dallington who then wagered and lost it to Matthew Palmer of Southwell—'in consequence of whose neglect', as the *Landed Gentry* records, 'the estate was impoverished'.

Like many loyal squires the Stauntons also suffered severely in the Civil War. Colonel William Staunton was fined more than £800 for having borne arms against Parliament. He returned home to a devastated house and a greatly reduced estate, but determined to maintain the family continuity. The coach-house has a datestone of '1655', the year before is death.

The male line of the Stauntons expired in 1688 on the death of the Colonel's son, Harvey, when the estate passed to

Staunton: a print by Laird of the north front in 1815.

Harvey's daughter, Anne, who had married a younger son of Sir Job Charlton, 1st Baronet, sometime Speaker of the House of Commons. Between about 1720 and 1790 Mrs Charlton's son, Job, MP for Newark, and his spinster daughter, Anne, made various improvements to Staunton Hall. As Mr Thorold observes, 'the family was not wealthy enough at that time to

pull down, and build a fashionable new house.'

Thus, outside, there is an engaging mixture of Tudor stone and Georgian brick, of mullioned and sash windows. Within, the old Great Hall was stylishly modernised in the 18th-century and the old screens passage given an 18th-century staircase. The dining-room in the Georgian bay of the west wing has a pleasant classical frieze and chimney-piece.

According to a somewhat optimistic family tradition, Carr of York is said to have had a hand in these Georgian embellishments. The architect is known to have done some work in the area; his name also cropped up in connection with the nearby seat of Carlton Hall.

Following the death of Miss Anne Charlton in 1807 Staunton was inherited by her cousin Elizabeth, the wife of the Reverend John Aspenshaw, who took the surname and arms of Staunton by Royal Licence. Their descendants were sporting

'squarsons' at Staunton for three generations. The third squarson was the most remarkable figure in Staunton's modern history, the late Reverend George Staunton.

As a boy George used some of the strings from the harp in the drawing-room to make rabbit snares. As a young man he worked in insurance but at the outbreak of the First World War he falsified his age from 42 to 38 and joined up in the ranks of the Royal Army Service Corps. He served at Ypres and won the Distinguished Conduct Medal before being invalided home in 1915. After the war, though he never attended a theological college, he entered Holy Orders and devoted himself to the care of his two parishes and four manors. He was cutting the grass in the churchyard at Staunton almost until his death aged 93 in 1965. The inscription on his gravestone reads, 'He did his best for the old name'.

The Reverend George Staunton was succeeded by his grandson, Edmund, the present squire. Born in 1943, he was educated at Eton and Cirencester and qualified as a land agent. He writes about agricultural matters, is an enthusiastic beagler (the Per Ardua Beagles meet at Staunton) and is currently chairman of the Nottinghamshire branch of the Country Landowners Association. He is also a past chairman of the county Farming and Wildlife Advisory Group. The 1,500-acre estate (a little less than half is farmed in hand) is notable for its conservation policy and Mr Staunton has planted many new trees.

Mr Staunton's wife, Elizabeth, is the daughter of the distinguished architect Peter Foster, surveyor of the fabric of Westminster Abbey. A folly designed by Mr Foster in the form of a classical temple is now being erected on the island between the ponds in the garden.

It is inspiring to report that the Stauntons, who have two sons (William and Robert), are continuing to do their 'best for the old name'.

Staunton Hall, near Orston, Nottinghamshire, is not open to the public though events are held occasionally (as advertised) to raise funds for the restoration of the church.

Staunton: the north (entrance) front.

CHARLTON
OF
HESLEYSIDE

Hesleyside: east front.

I N the 1850s that artistic and antiquarain couple Sir Walter and Lady Trevelyan of Wallington, in Northumberland, engaged young William Bell Scott to paint some canvases depicting representative episodes of Northumbrian life and history.

One of the scenes chosen shows a 16th-century Mrs Charlton serving up a large dish to the menfolk of Hesleyside, the family stronghold near Bellingham. As the dish is uncovered we see it contains not the expected roast but 'The Spur of the Charlton'.

The traditional significance of the spur is colourfully described in the late Air Commodore Lional Charlton's enjoyable edition of *The Recollections of a Northumbrian Lady 1815-1866* (Cape, 1949), being the memoirs of his grandmother, Barbara Charlton (*née* Tasburgh), whose husband, William, sat for the life-sized figure of his 16th-century ancestor and namesake in Scott's picture. The appearance of the spur intimated:

> that the larder was low, or that the young men were eager for a foray, or that a score needed to be wiped off; any plausible excuse, that is, for resort to boot and saddle, for an excursion over the Border, and for a homecoming laden with the spoils of war.

The Pre-Raphaelite style painting of *The Spur in the Dish* can still be seen at Wallington, which is now the property of the National Trust. Happily the actual spur, an iron relic of the late Elizabethan period with a long shank and a well-rowelled point, and indeed the Charltons themselves, remain at Hesleyside in the spectacularly wild and beautiful surroundings of North Tynedale.

This old Catholic family of Border squires have owned lands at Hesleyside and nearby Charlton, from which they take their surname, since the reign of Richard I in the second half of the 12th century. The first recorded occupier of a dwelling at Hesleyside was Edward Charlton in 1343. Then, this would have comprised a tower of rough stone for this was the time of fierce Border warfare.

In 1536 a later Edward Charlton of Hesleyside was well to the fore, together with the Scropes, Latimers, Lumleys and Percys, in the 'Pilgrimage of Grace', the noble if unavailing attempt to make Henry VIII restore the Catholic faith.

Right
Hesleyside: dining-room.

Edward's son, William, led the men of North Tynedale on less worthy missions. A notorious 'reiver', or cattle rustler, he took some 500 followers across the Border to Cavers where he is supposed to have captured the Ferrara sword, still at Hesleyside. The local tradition of 'The Spur of Charlton' also dates from the time of this William, who was commissioner for the enclosures on the Middle Marches.

Eventually, after James VI of Scotland had succeeded to the English throne, it became possible for the Border squires to live in unfortified houses. In 1631 Edward Charlton, later created a Baronet by Charles I for raising a troop of horse in the Civil War, built north and south wings, both two-storeyed, on the pele tower.

The baronetcy expired with Edward in 1674 and Hesleyside passed to his brother William, whose grandson and namesake set about improving the place in the early 18th century. Seemingly inspired by his education across the Channel at Douai, 'Runaway Will' (as he was known on account of his propensity for fleeing his creditors) added a third storey to the house and refaced the south front in a Frenchified manner. An arched passage for carriages was built running from the south front into the courtyard, where traces of the arches can be seen now that some Victorian accretions have been removed.

During this remodelling in about 1713, a priest's hiding hole was discovered in a chimneybreast. Like other Catholic families the Charltons were obliged to maintain a low profile and after Runaway Will's father had been tried for treason in 1689 they eschewed the Jacobite Risings. Nonetheless, a cousin, 'Bowerie' Charlton, previously pardoned by Queen

Left
Major and Mrs John Charlton with their son-in-law, Peter Loyd, and two of their grandchildren, on the staircase at Hesleyside.

Below
Hesleyside: south and east fronts.

Mrs John Charlton as a child in 1926
with some of the servants at
Hesleyside.

Anne for killing a Widdrington in a duel,
was 'out' in 1715.

Later in the 18th century the grounds
were handsomely landscaped in the manner of Capability Brown (a Northumbrian
by birth) and a small tower was built to
house a fine clock attributed to Hindley of
York Minster fame.

The other tower, the historic pele, met a
sad fate in the late 1790s when the formidable Mrs William Charlton (*née* Fenwick)
and her husband's trustees pulled it down,
using the stone to build new stables and
outhouses. The present Major John
Charlton has produced a charming tapes-
try which shows what Hesleyside must
have looked like before this gratuitious
piece of vandalism.

At the same time, on the credit side,
Mrs Charlton and the trustees remodelled
the east front, with its pleasing pediment.
The design of this late-Georgian facade is
said to have been one of the last works of
the Newcastle architect William Newton,
who died in 1798. The staircase, which
begins in one flight and branches out into
two, dates from the early 19th century.

In 1846 when William Charlton, a
pioneer of the railways, revered local
philanthropist and sportsman, took up
residence at Hesleyside, his wife, Barbara,
decided 'to make the house warmer and

more habitable'. The architect Ignatius
Bonomi (son of Joseph) was brought in to
make various alterations including the
rebuilding of the old clock tower, crowned
with an Italianate belvedere, and the
switching of the entrace from the east to
the north.

'The large hall, hitherto floored with
flags,' noted Barbara blithely, 'was pro-
perly floored to help counteract the un-
bearable cold, and converted into a
French drawing-room, beautifully decorated by Crace's foreman Worthington.'
The pretty painted ceiling of this elaborate interior (now the dining-room) is one
of the most charming features at
Hesleyside.

William and Barbara's younger son,

Right
Hesleyside: library.

800 acres are now farmed in hand (cattle-
and sheep-rearing) by their son-in-law,
Peter Loyd.

There are also 200 acres of woodland, at
least ten per cent of it newly planted.
Hesleyside's sporting tradition is main-
tained through the two local Border packs,

Far left
Hesleyside: staircase and landing.

Left
Hesleyside: courtyard.

Ernest, took the surname of Anne on
inheriting Burghwallis in Yorkshire from
Barbara's brother. In the present generation Ernest's grandson John, who served
in Burma and Normandy with the King's
Own Yorkshire Light Infantry, changed
is name back to Charlton after he had
married his cousin Mary ('Mamie') Charlton, the heiress of Hesleyside.

Over the past 36 years, since the arrival
of electricity, the Charltons have carried
out a thorough renovation and modernisation of the house and estate. Major
Charlton, who was High Sheriff of Northumberland in 1957 (exactly a century after
his and his wife's mutual great-grandfather), describes most of the 4,000-acre
property as 'dog and stick country', but

even though the grouse are now scarce and
the fishing in the North Tyne has been
ruined by the nearby Kielder Water
project.

The chapel at Hesleyside bears witness
to the family's steadfast adherence to the
old faith. The Charltons' young grandson
William, now at Ampleforth, has already
written an admirable history of this atmospheric seat.

The Charltons of Hesleyside are splendidly doughty champions of the privately-
owned heritage. 'We hope,' says the genial
Major, 'that our Border toughness will
enable us to withstand tax assaults on our
houses, as we discouraged the old enemy
from raiding our lands 400 years ago.' The
spur is surely there to survive.

*Hesleyside, Bellingham,
Northumberland, is not open
to the public, though the gardens are open occasionally
(as advertised) in aid of the
Red Cross.*

LEIGHTON OF LOTON

Right
Sir Michael Leighton, Bt, in his
Welsh kilt.

Right
Sir Michael Leighton, Bt, in his
Welsh kilt.

Above right
Loton Park, Shropshire: a
watercolour of the house, 1843.

Above right
Loton Park, Shropshire: a
watercolour of the house, 1843.

Below right
Loton: the north front.

Below right
Loton: the north front.

ACCUSTOMED to Scottish, and
even Irish, kilts, I was somewhat
surprised to discover Sir Michael
Leighton, 11th Baronet, the naturalist and
wildlife photographer, sporting a distinc-
tive Welsh kilt when I called to see Loton
Park, the Leighton family seat on the
Welsh Border. Sir Michael pointed out
that the National Welsh tartan was first
designed by Donald Richards of Abergele
in 1967. He is currently adopting his own
family tartan.

Although the long-established Leightons are of English origin, having been
seated in Shropshire since at least the 12th
century, Sir Michael descends from
numerous Welsh kings and princes
through his 15th-century ancestor's marriage to the great heiress Ankoret de
Burgh. Ankoret's grandmother, Elizabeth
Lady de Burgh, was the sister and heiress
of Foulk, Lord of Mawddwy in
Merioneth.

The Lords of Mawddwy were originally an independent Welsh tribe descended from Maredudd, Prince of Powys, son
of Bleddyn ap Cynfyn, King of Gwynedd
and Powys. Bleddyn acknowledged the
overlordship of Edward the Confessor
and was killed by Rhys ap Owain, King of
Deheubarth at Ystrad Tywi (or Powys
Castle) in 1075. Maredudd ap Bleddyn
reigned jointly with his brothers to begin
with, but managed to survive them all and
finally united all Powys under his rule in
the early 12th century.

In the 14th century Sir John de la Pole,
Lord of Mawddwy, married Elizabeth
Corbet, the daughter and heiress of Sir
Fulk Corbet from the old Shropshire
family seated at Watlesborough Castle
and Moreton Corbet. Eventually, Watlesborough passed to their daughter, Elizabeth de Burgh, and then on to her grand-
daughter, Ankoret, together with the
Welsh lordship of Bausley.

Left
Loton: south (entrance) front across
the cricket field.

Among the many manors Ankoret de Burgh brought to her husband, John Leighton, MP for Shropshire and an early adherent to the Tudor cause, was that of Loton ('The Reawood'), almost in Wales. The Leightons took their name from the manor of Leighton on the River Severn and were benefactors of Buildwas Abbey in the 12th and 13th centuries. In the late 14th century they came into the Church Stretton estate through marriage with the Cambrays.

Following the advantageous de Burgh marriage, the Leightons mainly lived at Watlesborough Castle in Shropshire. In the 16th century the family produced a succession of soldiers, courtiers, Sheriffs, MPs, and members of the Court of the Marches. Few families can match the Leighton record of 12 generations of MPs. At the Restoration of Charles II Robert Leighton, MP for Shrewsbury, was one of those selected for the abortive Order of 'Knights of the Oak'.

In the next generation, however, they acquired a baronetcy. It was the 2nd Baronet, Sir Edward Leighton, who switched the seat of the family from the old castle of Watlesborough to Loton in the reign of Queen Anne.

Left
Loton: saloon.

Right
Loton: theatre in east wing.

Far right
Loton: hall.

The manor house at Loton dates from about a century earlier, though much of what one sees today on the exterior of the impressively gabled south front is 19th-century 'Jacobean' rather than the real thing. The splendidly handsome north front of 11 bays with a segmental pediment in the centre and a part balustrade in the parapet was added in the early 18th century when Sir Edward took up residence.

The most notable 18th-century interior at Loton is the exquisite saloon with its oak panelling and pilasters. The Scots

Right
Loton: family portraits in library.

architect Robert Mylne, who also worked at Woodhouse not far away, carried out some alterations in 1773-74 and Edward Haycock is recorded as having made some improvements in 1819 for General Sir Baldwin Leighton, 6th Baronet.

The General had succeeded to the baronetcy earlier that year upon the death of his bachelor cousin Robert who, in 1806, had the distinction of escorting the Prince of Wales across the Border into his principality for the first time.

The gables and porch on the south front were erected to the design of Thomas Jones in 1838 by the 7th Baronet, another Sir Baldwin, a prominent politician who did much to improve the Loton estate. His

son and successor, christened Baldwyn for a change, married the de Tabley Warren heiress through whom Tabley in Cheshire (later a school) came into the family.

In 1873 Sir Baldwyn added the substantial east wing to the design of Bowdler of Shrewsbury. This contains a large private theatre. Adorned with a scientific collection of deer heads, it now serves as an auditorium for Sir Michael Leighton's copious cine-films of wildlife.

Sir Michael feels that he has inherited his love of the cine-camera from his colourful grandfather, Sir Bryan Leighton, 9th Baronet, soldier, sportsman and war correspondent, who filmed the Turkish forces in the Balkan War of 1913. He hunted his own pack of hounds and his wife was one of the first women Masters of Foxhounds in Great Britain.

Sir Bryan was also an intrepid airman, winning his wings with the Royal Flying Corps at the age of 45 and undertaking the first-ever parachute jump from less than 500 feet. Sir Bryan's two sons also joined him the RFC, the elder dying of wounds in 1917 and the younger, who was shot down by the 'Red Baron' von Richthofen, succeeding to the baronetcy in 1919.

In turn Sir Michael Leighton succeeded his father at the age of 22 in 1957. Today the 2,000-acre estate is well known for its conservation policies. There are some 1,300 acres of water-meadows, a deer park with a fallow deer herd, a wild-fowl sanctuary and 300 acres of woodland which Sir Michael has replanted. He has also relandscaped the gardens and laid out a new cricket pitch in front of the house where he performs regularly as a left-arm 'strike' bowler.

A passionate ornithologist, Sir Michael has recorded more than 120 wintering and nesting species at Loton and breeds barn owls. He has made a special study of the survival of the red kite in Wales. Whether kites or kilts, vintage cars, judging gun-dogs or writing poetry, Sir Michael Leighton's engaging enthusiasms certainly contribute to life on the Welsh Border.

Loton Park, Alberbury, Shropshire, is not open to the public though the National Speed Hill Climb is occasionally held in the park.

O'CONOR OF CLONALIS

Mr and Mrs Pyers O'Conor Nash and their children.

IN 1186 the last effective High King of Ireland, Rory O'Connor, whose family had been Kings of Connacht, (or Connaught) since the 4th century, was forced to surrender sovereignty over those territories occupied by the Norman invaders. Eight hundred years later, it is good to report that some, at least 700 acres, of the family lands by the River Suck in Co Roscommon remain in the ownership of the O'Conors. (The crack is that this senior surviving branch of the family spell their surname thus because they could 'never make "n's" meet'.) Uniquely among the ancestral seats of Ireland, Clonalis House near Castlerea, home of Pyers and Marguerite O'Conor Nash and their family, still celebrates a tradition that has nobly remained Gaelic and Roman Catholic.

Although the present building, erected for the then O'Conor Don chief by the architect Frederick Pepys Cockerell, goes back only to 1878, the remarkable objects on show to the visitor represent a veritable microcosm of Irish history. Outside the Italianate entrance front, for instance, is displayed the Coronation Stone of the Kings of Connaught which dates from Druidic times. The chosen candidate, having laid aside his sword in favour of 'a straight white hazel wand as a sceptre and an emblem of purity and rectitude', would place his foot on this very stone which still bears an ancient footprint.

In the typical roomy and comfortable F. Pepys Cockerell interior is a cornucopia of antiquities. As our illustration of the library shows, these include such items as a

Clonalis, Co Roscommon: garden front.

vellum pedigree of the O'Conors stretching ambitiously back to Milesius in the 5th century BC; a 17th-century chalice (cleverly designed to come apart for ease of concealment in penal times) and a penal cross; and a handful of the 100,000 historic documents from the Clonalis archives which range from parchment containing the last recorded verdicts under the old Brehon law to a letter from Anthony Trollope in his days as a post-office surveyor in Ireland. Dominating the picture is the stringless harp of O'Carolan, the last of the great Irish bards.

This blind harpist, whose portrait can be glimpsed on the left of the pedigree in

Clonalis: the library, with O'Carolan's harp.

Clonalis: entrance hall.

the photograph, enjoyed the patronage of the O'Conor family in the early 18th century. One day at Belanagare, not far from Clonalis, the bard observed, 'When I am among the O'Conors, the harp has the old sound in it'.

Two of O'Carolan's airs were dedicated to the family—*Charles O'Conor of Belanagare* and *Denis O'Conor*. In 1720, Denis, rendered destitute by the forfeitures in the wake of the Williamite Wars, walked barefoot to Dublin in order to recover a small portion of his property in the courts. 'Don't be impudent to the poor,' he would admonish his sons. 'I was the son of a gentleman but you were sons of a ploughman.'

Charles O'Conor of Belanagare, Denis's son, was one of the greatest upholders of the traditional picture of Ireland as the Land of Saints and Scholars. An antiquary and author of *Dissertations on the History of Ireland*, he was responsible for collecting the bulk of the highly important Irish archives on display in the old billiard room at Clonalis.

One display case in this room records the career of Charles O'Conor's great-grandson and namesake, a successful lawyer who became the first Roman Catholic candidate to run for the presidency of the United States. Another member of the family to distinguish himself outside Ireland was the diplomatist Sir Nicholas O'Conor. During his stint as British Ambassador to the sultan of Turkey, he apparently took exception to the Sultan's demand that the Imperial presence be approached through a tunnel on all fours. Sir Nicholas duly emerged from the aperture stern first.

In 1820 the antiquary's grandson, Owen Conor, MP, a close friend and coadjutor of Daniel O'Connell, 'the Liberator' and champion of Catholic emancipation, succeeded his bachelor kinsman, Alexander, as head of the family and as O'Conor Don. The old Kingdom of Connaught had been divided in 1385 between two cousins: O'Conor Don and O'Conor Roe. After the destruction of Ballintober Castle, the family stronghold a few miles away, the O'Conor Dons settled at Clonalis where, by the early 18th century, they had built a double gable-ended house.

By the time the Belanagare branch of the O'Conors succeeded to the Clonalis estate a century later, the house, in its low-lying position close to the River Suck, was coming to be regarded as unhealthy. Accordingly, in the time of Owen's grandson, the Right Honourable Charles Owen O'Conor Don, MP—another famous figure in Irish history who gained recognition for the Gaelic language on school curricula and was the prime mover in the foundation of University College, Dublin—the old house was abandoned, finally to be wrecked in a storm in 1961.

Between 1878 and 1880 the O'Conor Don built the present Clonalis House on a more elevated site affording views of the majestic parkland. Cockerell, his architect, represented the third generation of a noted architectural dynasty; he was the son of the neo-classicist C. R. Cockerell (of Ashmolean and Fitzwilliam Museum fame) and grandson of Samuel Pepys Cockerell, who was himself great-grandnephew to Samuel Pepys, the diarist.

For the design of the new Clonalis, Cockerell adopted a style that, as Mark

Bence-Jones has pointed out, comes half-way between Victorian Italianate and the 'Queen Anne' which Norman Shaw was making so popular in England at this period. Unlike Shaw's 'Queen Anne' houses, though, Clonalis is faced in cement rather than brick.

The interior is considerably easier on the eye. The handsome hall, with the Standard of Ireland carried at George V's Coronation by the O'Conor Don of the day (a well-known shot) has Ionic columns of pink Mallow marble. The black marble chimney-piece in the dining-room has flanking niches for turf—a feature also used by Cockerell in his stone Tudor-Revival chimney-pieces at Blessingbourne, Co Tyrone.

The present incumbent of Clonalis, Pyers O'Conor Nash, is a nephew of the late O'Conor Don, a Jesuit priest whose photograph beside the Cross of Cong (commissioned by Turlough Moor O'Conor, High King of Ireland, 1123) is displayed in the library. Since 1981 Pyers and his wife, Marguerite (née Egan), have been carrying out a thorough and sympathetic restoration of the house and estate. About half the land is farmed (arable) and there are 120 acres of woodland, useful for the occasional shooting party.

Mr O'Connor Nash, a former barrister and merchant banker, succeeded the Knight of Glin in 1985 as chairman of the Historic Houses and Gardens Association (HITHA), and is a leading campaigner for the conservation of the endangered Irish heritage.

Clonalis House, Castlerea, Co Roscommon, is open to the public during weekends in May, June and September and daily in July and August.

Some of the items in the lace exhibition.

EYSTON OF HENDRED

Mr Thomas Eyston and his mother, Lady Agnes Eyston.

THE pretty villages of East and West Hendred under the Berkshire Downs—now absurdly placed, under the odious Heath-Walker boundary changes of the 1970s, in Oxfordshire—take much care to preserve their architectural heritage. Among the local residents is that key 'heritage' figure Jennifer Jenkins (she and her husband, Lord Jenkins of Hillhead the politician, live in East Hendred), formerly chairman of the Historic Buildings Council and now of the National Trust. Hendred House is the family seat of the Eystons, that epitome of the 'OCF' (Old Catholic Family) so beloved of Evelyn Waugh and other romantic admirers of recusancy.

The Tridentine Mass is still celebrated every day in the private chapel of the old manor house (where they have been seated since medieval times) by a priest living *en famille* in the best Catholic traditions. Inevitably having to maintain a low profile through the penal times, the Eystones emerged after Catholic Emancipation to be public-spirited squires (Deputy Lieutenants, Justices of the Peace, High Sheriffs), while remaining loyal servants and benefactors of the old faith. They have intermarried with other distinguished Catholic dynasties such as the Beringtons, Fitzherberts, Huddlestons, Petres, Blounts and the Metcalfes, lineal descendants of the great St Thomas More,

Opposite
Hendred House, Oxfordshire: view across Italian-style garden.

the 'man for all seasons' who defied Henry VIII.

The visitor to East Hendred may find himself confused by the number of ecclesiastical buildings connected with the Eystons. Champs Chapel, built by Carthusian monks, has recently been restored as a musuem. St Augustine's, the present Anglican church, still has the pre-Reformation Eyston Chapel, built as a chantry by the family in the late 15th century. St Mary's, built by Charles Eyston in 1865, to the designs of Charles Buckler, is an exceptionally good Victorian Catholic church.

The history of the private chapel (dedicated to St Amand) in the old manor house itself goes back to the mid-13th century when Sir John de Turbervile obtained permission to build it from Pope Alexander IV. The manor later passed by marriage and descent from the Turberviles first to the Arches family and then to the Stowes. In the 1440s, Isabel Stowe, the heiress of East Hendred (then an important centre of the flourishing wool and cloth trades) married John Eyston, the direct male line ancestor of the present Lord of the Manor of Arches, Abbey Manor and Catmore, Thomas More Eyston.

Little is known about Hendred during the years of persecution. The manor house became know as a Mass Centre, with a priest's hole in the roof next to the chapel, as also did Catmore, another property on the Eyston estate, half a dozen miles off on the Downs, whither the family had to flee on occasions. St Amand's chapel apparently became a woodshed and Mass must have been celebrated in the gallery. Following the restoration of the chapel during the reign of James II, it was promptly sacked by 'Dutch William's' troops *en route* for Oxford in 1689.

Architecturally, Hendred is a typical medieval manor house with a Great Hall in the middle, two wings at either side and a chapel at the back. Various additions have been made to this basic structure down the ages. Recently, however, there has been a radical tidying-up operation that has meant the removal of many of the 19th-century accretions.

A drawing hanging in the dining-room shows the entrace front as it was in about 1700, with four sets of gables. Until a few years ago a large late-Georgian block, quite out of proportion with the front of the house, faced on to the east garden. The latter extension was then demolished and

the present courtyard created.

At the same time a spacious new drawing-room was imaginatively constructed out of the old larders and the Great Hall, Hendred's finest feature, was transformed to its present superb state. The old fireplace, rediscovered in the village, was reinstated in its rightful position; the false ceiling stripped away to reveal the glorious roof, with its hammerbeams and arched trusses. The Great Hall makes a splendid setting for the family portraits (formerly in the demolished lateGeorgian dining-room) dominated by a copy of Holbein's celebrated group of the Mores.

The present squire pays tribute to the work of the architect David Nye during this extensive renovation and, especially, to his mother, Lady Agnes Eyston, for her aesthetic hand in the proceedings. Lady Agnes, an aunt of the present Earl of Mexborough, also relandscaped the gardens, which have an exquisitely Italian flavour.

Thomas Eyston's father and namesake died of wounds while serving with the Royal Berkshire Regiment in Belgium in 1940 when the Lord of the Manor was eight. His younger brother, Jack, lives at the Elizabethan Mapledurham House on the Thames (inherited through the Blount connection) with his wife, Lady Anne (*née* Maitland), and family; the two Eyston sisters are both nuns. Tom Eyston, a bachelor, was educated at Ampleforth and read estate management at Trinity College, Cambridge. The whole of the 2,800-acre estate is in hand (beef, cattle and sheep) and some 28 people are employed. There are two shoots on the estates, one of which the squire runs as a private syndicate, as well as deer stalking.

Mr Eyston occasionally opens the house in aid of repairs to St Amand's Roman Catholic School in East Hendred, whose foundation stone he laid in 1962. The school had been endowed a century earlier by his great-grandfather, one of a long line of cultivated Catholic squires.

Above
Hendred: library.

Opposite
Hendred: Great Hall.

Hendred House, East Hendred, near Wantage, Oxfordshire, is not normally open to the public.

FETHERSTONHAUGH-FRAMPTON OF MORETON

Moreton House, Dorset.

LAWRENCE of Arabia, who was buried at Moreton in Dorset in 1935 predicted that his bones would receive some rattling after his death. Amid the recent outbreak of bone-rattling, an interesting point was missed about T. E. Lawrence's connection with his place of burial.

The choice of Moreton was not based simply on its proximity to his cottage at Clouds Hill near Bovington Camp, but was in accordance with his mother's wish that he should be laid to rest in a place of family association. Although Lawrence himself was illegitimate, his undoubted father, Sir Thomas Chapman, an Irish baronet, was related to the Squire of Moreton, the Fetherstonhaugh-Framptons, who knew the hero of the desert as 'Cousin Ned'.

The Framptons acquired the estate more than 600 years ago when Walter de Frampton, of a family settled near Weymouth, married heiress of the manor of Moreton, Margaret, whose maiden name is supposed to have been Husee. Their son, John, was MP for Dorset and said to be present at Agincourt. His successors at Moreton appear to have done little of note until Robert Frampton, High Sheriff of Dorset in the year of Queen Elizabeth I's accession, built a Tudor manor house on the property in 1580.

There survives at Moreton a small drawing of this building which was demolished some time in the early 18th century. Park House (as the smaller part of the present house is called) has some stone mullioned windows which may have come from old Tudor manor.

The best-known member of this Dorset dynasty was Robert's great-nephew, the colourful sportsman Tregonwell Frampton, Keeper of the Running Horses to four sovereigns (William III, Queen Anne and the first two Georges) and nicknamed the 'Father of the Turf'.

Tregonwell is said to have travelled from Waddock (where he lived in a farmhouse on the Moreton estate) to Newmarket (where he raced and gambled merrily until his death, aged 88, in 1729) with his luggage carried by mule train. The endearingly equine features—and extraordinary eyebrows—of this bachelor absentee squire now dominate the front hall at Moreton.

The present house was built by Tregonwell's cousin, James Frampton, to whose father the old reprobate had conveyed the estate. First, in 1742, James erected the part now known as Park House—originally the 'offices' (nurseries, kitchens, servant's quarters, and so on). There was probably an old cottage on this particular site—the only visible trace of which is a small window, though parts of a former staircase were uncovered when a floor was taken up during some alterations in the 1960s.

Next he built the classically simple main block with its centre bay breaking forward under a pediment. No record exists of the designer or craftsmen connected with this most delightful Palladian structure in Portland ashlar; James's diary merely states that he built the house in 1744, furnished it in 1745 and married Mary Houlton of Farleigh Castle in Somerset in 1746.

Mary died childless in 1762 and James put up a splendid marble tablet by Peter Van Gelder to her memory in the church

Opposite
Moreton: entrance front.

in the park which he had rebuilt in the 1730s. His second wife, Phyllis, was the widow of George III's physician, Charlton Wollaston (whose death was said to be 'occasioned by opening a mummy, he having previously by accident cut his finger'). They had two children and to accommodate the growing family James added some 13 feet to the south-east side of the house. This 1799 extension included the insertion of a large bow window in the dining-room.

Happily few further changes of any significance have been made to Moreton House, an 18th-century gem, during the last 200 years. The hall has its original plasterwork panels, swags and garlands; the library still contains the lusciously carved overdoor and window base.

The outstanding 'Adamesque' ceiling of the drawing-room (one of the many rooms to be affected by the extension of 1799) is rather in the style of John Flaxman, while the chimney-piece seems

Moreton: view through library to drawing-room.

similar to Van Gelder's work on Mary Frampton's memorial tablet in the church. The cantilevered staircase and wrought-iron balustrade date from 1744. The window was glazed with stained glass but most of it was destroyed when a bomb fell near the house in 1941.

An earlier bomb devastated the windows of the church, but their exceptional replacements by that modern master of engraved glass, Laurence Whistler, has made St Nicholas's at Moreton one of the sights of Dorset. Apart from Whistler's artistry, the fireplace in the Frampton pew evokes a satisfying picture of squire-archical comfort.

The estate diaries of Moreton's builder, James Frampton, provide an entertaining record of 18-century country life. In a preface written to his son, namesake and successor shortly before his death in 1784, James observed that his

> general plan, besides rebuilding the old Family mansion, etc, has been by some few purchases, and ornamenting the Estate, round it, to contribute towards making the whole as complete as the nature of the Country would well admit of, rather than Large ... with which if providence has endowed you with a good share of common sense, as I happily believe, you may pass through life with great comfort, credit and independence ...

The second James Frampton of Moreton was called upon to exercise his 'common sense' when, in 1834, as the local magistrate, he was obliged to arrest the so-called 'Tolpuddle martyrs' and to send them on to trial.

His wife, Lady Harriot Fox-Strang-ways, daughter of the 2nd Earl of Ilchester, recorded a more amusing incident in Moreton's history about the occasion when Princess Charlotte, George IV's ill-fated daughter, came to the house in 1814 and spotted an engraving of 'Prinny' which was unfortunately cracked. 'On perceiving this print', related Lady Harriot, she exclaimed:

> 'Is this the way in which you treat my Father and your future King!' and seizing it in her hand declared she would carry it away with her but of course forgot and left it in the Drawing Room.

In 1855 the Frampton heiress of Moreton, Louisa, married Rupert Fetherstonhaugh from County Meath and they took the name Fetherstonhaugh-Frampton. Their son, Harry, High Sheriff of the county in 1929 and a celebrated West Country sportsman who was Master of the Cattistock and the South Dorset, considerably reduced the family property by selling the Briantspuddle and Affpuddle estates to the Debenhams.

Today the Moreton estate, owned by a family trust, is just less than 3,000 acres in extent, mostly let. There is a private shooting syndicate, let deer-stalking, and three miles of fishing on the Frome.

Harry's son, Commander Roger Fetherstonhaugh-Frampton, a Deputy Lieutenant for Dorset, and his wife, Bridget, whose parents, Sir Mansfeldt and Lady Findlay, formerly rented Moreton House from the family are now sadly both dead. The Commander and his wife had carried out a thorough renovation of the house in the 1950s.

Two of their four daughters now live at Moreton: Mary, and Philippa, the wife of Major Donald Hobbs, who has four children. Mary Fetherstonhaugh-Frampton, the eldest daughter, has been clerk in charge of the office of the Serjeant at Arms in the House of Commoms and was appointed MBE in 1967.

She is an enthusiastic moderniser of cottages on the Moreton estate, and her local activities have included membership of the Winfrith Heath Committee fighting the Central Electricity Generating Board power station which threatens to disfigure this sleepy corner of south-east Dorset immortalised by Thomas Hardy as 'Egdon Heath'.

Moreton House, Moreton, Dorchester, Dorest, is not open to the public though sponsored rides in the park are occasionally held in aid of the Save the Children Fund.

Below
Portrait of Tregonwell Frampton, Keeper of the Running Horses to four sovereigns.

Below
Miss Mary Fetherstonhaugh-Frampton.

MYNORS OF TREAGO

Sir Roger and Lady Mynors (left) and Sir Humphrey and Lady Mynors (right).

Opposite
Treago, Herefordshire: from the south-east.

VARIOUS solutions have been put forward as to the future of country houses, among them the proposal by Auberon Waugh, a staunch critic of the 'evils of primogeniture', that they should be filled to the rafters with relations. There is a happy arrangement at Treago, in the Welsh Marches, a romantic manor house that lies in a hollow at St Weonards, near Ross-on-Wye in Herefordshire. It is the home of both the eminent classicist Sir Roger Mynors, his twin brother, Sir Humphrey Mynors, who is an equally eminent figure in the City of London, and their respective wives.

The Mynorses of Treago have enjoyed one of the longest tenures of squire-archical dynasties in Herefordshire. Philip Mynors is recorded as 'of Treago' (otherwise *Tre-iago*, which means the place of home of James) in the first half of the 15th century, though there is no evidence of any building work earlier than the latter part of that century. Treago (listed Grade II★) is basically a square stone fortified house, with a tower at each corner, which was altered several times in the 17th, 18th and 19th centuries.

The builder of Treago was probably Philip's son, Richard, a prominent administrator in South Wales in the last quarter of the 15th century and Sheriff of Herefordshire in 1500. He certainly built the north aisle of St Weonard's church

Treago: Tower Room.

and the medievalist A. J. Taylor has pointed out that some of the ubiquitous mason's marks on the stones of Treago are also to be found on the work of Richard Mynors's chief, William Herbert, 1st Earl of Pembroke, at Raglan Castle.

Richard Mynors's eldest son, Roger, was knighted in 1527 after many years as Henry VIII's Serjeant of the Cellar, but he and his Derbyshire heiress wife, Alice Knyfton, did not have children and Treago passed to his younger brother, Thomas, who committed suicide there with 'a certain knife of the value of one penny' in 1539.

There is an old 'Pope's hole' in the north-east tower at Treago and the Mynorses seem to have remained Catholics until about the time of the Civil War when, following several convictions for recusancy, Rowland Mynors conformed. In 1610 he had made an unusually grand marriage for a Herefordshire squire at Wollaton, the mighty (if then encumbered) seat of the Willoughbys in Nottinghamshire.

From her portrait in the dining-room at Treago, Theodosia, his bride, looks a distinctly formidable personality. In honour of this impressive alliance, Willoughby became a family Christian name.

The substantial alterations made to Treago in about 1670 can be attributed to

Rowland and Theodosia's son, Robert. These included a staircase in the north-east, several bedroom floors and the pretty plaster ceiling in what is now the back kitchen. The handsome barn has a sundial dated 1664.

The next significant changes occurred a century later following the death of the last Mynors of the male line (who had taken his maternal name of Gouge). Robert Mynors Gouge's widow, Mary, married Charles Morgan, a younger son of the Tredegar family, and he added the remarkable projecting upper storey to the south-east tower. Inside is a circular smoking room, the Tower Room, with its contemporary Gothic decoration.

Mary Morgan, whose second husband succeeded to Tredegar in 1771, bequeathed Treago to her first husband's kinsman, Peter Rickards of Evenjobb in Radnorshire, on condition that he took the name of Mynors. Thus, as so often happens in the histories of landed dynasties, the family continuity was preserved—if somewhat precariously in the first instance (Peter's grand-daughter recorded that he 'had kept open house at Treago and a pack of hounds at his own expense' and 'very seriously injured the property').

In the early 19th century the Rickards Mynors became principally based over the Welsh border in Radnorshire where Peter's son and namesake built Evancoyd. However, when his own son was grown up, this second Peter returned to Treago.

Before moving back in the mid-1840s Peter Rickards Mynors made substantial changes to the building whose former appearance can be seen in Thomas Tudor's two sketches, drawn some 20 years previously, now hanging in the drawing-room. A new front entrance was built to the east, approached by a grandiose carriage drive; Tudor-cum-Gothic style windows were inserted; and, in order to provide extra living space, the original internal central courtyard (with its deep well) was roofed over. Other early-Victorian works at Treago included the walled kitchen garden, the stables and the remodelling of the barn.

Over the next 100 years Treago was frequently let out. By the time Roger Mynors inherited the place in 1940 from an independent-minded spinster cousin (first of her sex to climb the Matterhorn in winter), the estate was in a sorry plight. The house had neither electricity nor running water.

Ever since, the whole revenue from the 1,000-acre estate (let to four tenant-farmers) and a considerable amount of capital have been put into its improvement. The woodland has been replanted and extended (to 120 acres), while the house has been given a thorough overhaul. The entire roof has been reslated and insulated and water, electricity and central heating installed.

Three of the blocked windows were reopened and various discoveries included four quadrant braces among the lumber which were reinstated in the hammer-beam roof of the original early-Tudor Great Hall. The Mynorses pay tribute to the gardener and his wife, Jack and Evelyn Meademore, for their key part in the resuscitation of the family seat.

In the 1950s Treago was the last home of the Very Reverend Cyril Alington, the former Dean of Durham, and his wife. One of their daughters, Lavinia, married Roger Mynors; another, Elizabeth, is the wife of Lord Home of the Hirsel, the former Prime Minster. The Dean had his own chapel in an upper room at Treago; while the Tower Room witnessed the completion of the new translation of *The Book of Job* by Roger Mynors, one of the team that produced *The New English Bible*.

A distinguished scholar, Roger Mynors was knighted in 1963 and retired from the Corpus Christi Professorship of Latin Language and Literature at Oxford seven years later when he and his wife settled permanently at Treago. They were joined by Sir Humphrey Mynors and his wife Lydia, daughter of the historian and archaeologist Professor Sir Ellis Minns. Sir Humphrey, originally an economics don at Cambridge, went on to become deputy governor of the Bank of England and the first chairman of the Panel on Takeovers and Mergers in the City. Today he applies his financial acumen to the Treago accounts.

In 1964 Sir Humphrey received a baronetcy—one of the last (or so it seems) to be created. The heir to the title is Richard Mynors, director of music at Merchant Taylor's School, Crosby, who is married to another well-known churchman's daughter, Fiona Reindorp. From time to time Sir Humphrey and Lady Mynors's five children and 14 grandchildren help fill this familial seat.

Treago, St Weonards, Herefordshire, though not open to the public as a general rule, is shown by appointment and also during the annual village fête.

Treago: dining-room.

HENEAGE OF HAINTON

Hainton Hall: west front.

THE popular image of Lincolnshire is a flat, intensively farmed county, but a tour round the beautiful Hainton estate, not far from the cathedral city of Lincoln, with its owner James Heneage reveals a different picture. More than half the 5,500-acre estate is in the Lincolnshire wolds Area of Outstanding Natural Beauty (for once an accurate description) and the place has a striking diversity of untouched habitats.

Mr Heneage, who farms some 2,000 acres in-hand, is an enthusiastic conservationist. The estate includes a Site of Special Scientific Interest, Beniworth Haven, consisting of two lakes, woodland and grassland, and a recent survey of the rest of the property by the Lincolnshire and South Humberside Trust for Nature Conservation found it 'of high conservation value'.

The old hedgerows have remained largely intact, resulting in a landscape that, as the survey points out, is 'attractive to look at and rich in all aspects of natural history'. Even though the majority of the estate is now arable, there are few fields of more than 30 acres and there are more than 400 acres of woods planted for sport. There is a flourishing shoot at Hainton with two 'keepers.

The Trust's survey recorded an encouraging number of birds, including such less usual species as the lesser-spotted woodpecker, wheatear, sand martin and barn owl. There are several rookeries on the estate and a bank in an old sandpit had nesting sand martins. Other nesting birds recorded were wren, treecreeper and skylark.

Mr Heneage's agricultural enterprise consists of 800 breeding mule ewes and a rotation of wheat, peas and oilseed rape. Since inheriting Hainton from his cousin, Lord Heneage, he has more than doubled the land in-hand and carried out a major overhaul of the Hall and the estate.

Born in 1945, the only son of the late Lieutenant-Colonel Neil Heneage (who died in 1953), Mr Heneage was educated at Ampleforth and Cirencester. Before coming back to Hainton at the end of the 1960s he went round the world, working in Australia and South America and gained useful experience as a land agent. He is a member of the Lincolnshire Country Landowners Association executive committee, of Timber Growers UK and of the Royal Forestry Society, which has had open days in the Hainton woods.

He is active in the life of the county, serving as High Sheriff, and is a member of the Lincoln Cathedral Appeal committee. Mr Heneage married Roberta Wilkinson from Sussex in 1978. They have two sons, Christopher and William, and a daughter, Phoebe.

Since the early 1970s there have been a series of dramatic changes to the appearance of Hainton Hall. To reduce the risk of recurring dry rot, which had wreaked havoc at Hainton in the 1950s and 1960s, Mr Heneage had the top floor of the west front taken off. The stucco was removed to reveal traces of the old red-brick underneath. Then, with the help of architect James Hemmings, of Stamford, a new entrance facade was created with new bricks, handmade to the old pattern discovered underneath the stucco, and handsome sash windows instead of the previous plate glass.

Opposite
Hainton: dining-room.

A couple of years ago a remarkable octagon designed by Charles Morris was added to the east. This contains a new kitchen and a smaller dining-room. The magnificent main dining-room was originally the hall. The drawing room has been stylishly redecorated for the first time in more than a century.

The interiors of Hainton are noted for their Georgian splendour. The dining-room, for example, rises to two storeys in height with giant fluted pilasters of the Ionic order, a goodly ceiling and a chimney-piece with caryatids in profile. The morning room has particularly fine overdoors with broken voluted pediments that are evocative of James Gibbs. The staircase, lit by a large Venetian window, is approached through a screen of Ionic columns and the ceiling is adorned with rococo plasterwork. The upper landing has a tripartite Ionic arcade.

The present house dates from 1638 (which is the year on a datestone in the attractive stone south front) though the Heneages have been seated at Hainton since the 14th century. The estate seems to have been put together in the reign of Edward III by John Heneage.

The family were to the fore in the 16th century when Sir Thomas Heneage was Keeper of the Privy Purse and Groom of the Stole to Henry VIII and his nephew and namesake was Vice-Chamberlain to Elizabeth I. It is recorded that the elder St Thomas was present with Henry at the 'winning of Bulloyne'.

Another nephew of Sir Thomas's, Sir George, succeeded to Hainton in 1553. Sir George was MP for Grimsby, Vice-Admiral of Lincolnshire and prominent in the suppression of the rebels during the bloody Elizabethan campaigns in Ireland. He is commemorated in an exceptionally fine monument, with exquisite alabaster hands at prayer, in the Heneage chapel in Hainton church.

There are two churches in the grounds of Hainton. The Anglican church has a handsome clock, recently installed by James Heneage, who himself worships with his family in the Catholic chapel on the other side of the stables. This Gothic chapel, which serves as the Catholic parish church for Market Rasen nearby, was designed in 1836 by the Lincoln architect Edward James Willson for Mrs G. F. Heneage (*née* Tasburgh), a Catholic.

During the Civil War the then squire Sir George Heneage ('George the second' for ease of identification in the family tree) seems to have sat on the fence—a wise

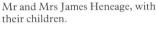

Mr and Mrs James Heneage, with their children.

programme which took in the school (still in use by a playgroup chaired by Roberta Heneage), the Heneage Arms public house, the kennels, and several farms and cottages. There were special opportunities for Heneage and Willson to spread themselves as the layout of the village was changed by the alteration of a turnpike road. As a result Hainton is an important example of Willson's work, both Gothic and Georgian.

Both George the ninth and his elder son, Edward Heneage, were Members of Parliament. Edward went on to become Chancellor of the Duchy of Lancaster and was created a peer in 1896. He added a porch by William Burn in 1875. The Barony passed in turn to his two bachelor sons. George the tenth (a sportsman and chairman of the Lindsey County Council) and Thomas (a clergyman in British Columbia), before expiring in 1967.

The next head of the family, Sir Arthur Heneage, who was MP for Louth for more than 20 years and celebrated for the Heneage Report on water, lived at Walesby Hall nearby. Meanwhile Hainton itself had been a cause of concern for the trustees of the estate. To reduce costs, part of the house had been demolished in 1954. The east wing disappeared and the

Hainton as it was at the end of the 19th century.

move in a county riven between Royalists and Parliamentarians. Shortly before the outbreak of the war, Sir George began building the present house.

Following his death in 1659 the estate passed from father to son, George to George, until 1745 when George the sixth was succeeded by his nephew George the seventh, whose mother was a Fieschi of a family of Genoese counts. George the seventh brought in Capability Brown to landscape the park in 1763.

George the eighth remodelled the house to the designs of Peter Atkinson Junior (son of the Carr of York's assistant) in about 1807. Atkinson's work consisted principally of rebuilding and heightening the west wing and building the impressive stables.

George the ninth, for whose wife Willson built the Catholic chapel, was a model improving Victorian landlord. He employed Willson as his estate architect from 1835 to 1854 on an ambitious building

top floor of the south wing was removed. The architect Donald Insall also scraped off the stucco from the south front to reveal the attractive old stone.

Mr Heneage recalls that in the 1950s and 1960s there was not one bit of the house which did not have to be treated for dry rot. To have arrested the house's decline and then to have achieved an ambitious new remodelling in the way he has is praiseworthy.

'My main object in life', says this determined young Lincolnshire squire, 'is to hand Hainton on to my successor as a going concern.'

Group appointments to visit the Hainton estate near Lincoln will be favourably considered and local events are held occasionally (as advertised).

47

HOUISON CRAUFURD OF CRAUFURDLAND

Craufurdland Castle, Ayrshire: view of garden front from the valley below.

AMONG the longest-established landowners in Scotland are the Houison Craufurds of Craufurdland in the old county of Ayrshire. They trace their descent from John Craufurd of Craufurdland, who appears to have had the estate (previously known as Ardoch) conveyed to him by his father, Sir Reginald de Craufurd, Sheriff of Ayre and husband of the Loudoun heiress, in the early 13th century. The present laird, Peter Houison Craufurd, has recently opened the family seat, Craufurdland Castle near Kilmarnock, to the public by appointment.

The oldest part of the castle, the tower to the right of the present entrance front, traditionally goes back to the 12th century. McGibbon and Ross's study of *Castellated and Domestic Architecture in Scotland* dampeningly dates the architecture of the tower to about 1500, but it seems only fair to suppose that the tower must incorporate part of the original 'keep' built on the splendid defensive site perched high above the Craufurdland Water in the picturesque valley below.

The next oldest part of the castle dates from the 1640s. Best seen from the back, this atmospheric wing to the east of the main block has three crow-stepped gables

Opposite
Craufurdland: entrance front.

48

and, inside, in what is known as the King's Room on the first floor, a notable ceiling displays the arms of Charles I (dated 1648, just before his execution).

Prints and drawings in the castle indicate that this 17th-century wing was, in fact, built as a mansion house quite separate from the old tower to the west. The gap in the middle was filled with a dramatic vengeance in the third stage of Craufurdland's building history when the castle acquired its present imposing appearance in the early 19th century. With its massive central tower and arched Gothic doorway, the castellated Craufurdland is rather reminiscent of a church.

The Craufurd family history reveals a proud record of resistance to the dreaded Sassenachs. James Craufurd helped his kinsman, the dashing patriot Sir William Wallace, become Warden of Scotland in 1297; his grandson, Sir William Craufurd, was wounded fighting the English in France at the Battle of Crevelt in 1423; a subsequent laird was killed at Flodden.

Even though the last of the direct male line of the Craufurds of Craufurdland, John Walkinshaw Craufurd, joined the British Army in the 18th century, he showed his true Scottish spirit when the Earl of Kilmarnock was beheaded for being 'out' in the 1745 Jacobite Rising. Craufurd attended his noble neighbour on the scaffold and is said to have held a corner of the cloth which received the unfortunate peer's severed head. For this act of loyal friendship, Craufurd's name was apparently placed at the bottom of the Army List.

Crauford curiously settled the estate, on his deathbed in 1793, upon the banker Thomas Coutts, but the laird's aunt, Elizabeth Houison, was not having any of this. She successfully contested Coutts's inheritance and in 1806 the House of Lords established her as the next laird of Craufurdland. Her husband, John Houison, was himself the proprietor of Braehead in Midlothian, a property traditionally granted to his ancestor by James II after an incident that is part of Scottish folklore.

The story goes that James II, travelling incognito (as was his wont) in the neighbourhood of Cramond Bridge near Edinburgh, was set upon by a gang of ruffians but happily rescued by Jock Houison, a local husbandman who afterwards took the anonymous victim to 'his humble dwelling' for a wash-and-brush-up. Before taking his leave, the mysterious stranger invited the worthy Houison to look him up in Edinburgh Castle—asking for 'Ane James Stewart'.

The best-known version of this yarn was told (albeit featuring James V, rather than the more likely James II) by Sir Walter Scott in his *Tales of a Grandfather*. This burnisher of romantic Scottish traditions duly ensured that, when George IV paid his famous visit to Holyrood in 1822, (wearing flesh-coloured tights under his kilt), Jock's descendant was in attendance with a silver basin for His Majesty to wash his hands. Performing the ceremony was Elizabeth Houison's grandson, William Houison Craufurd, laird of Braehead and of Craufurdland, where he carried out the extensive remodelling of the castle in 1825.

The '*Servitium Lavacri*' has continued as one of the quaintest ceremonies connected with the Crown. At the beginning of each reign, the proprietor of Braehead performs this 'Act of Service' to his sovereign in return for his continued tenure of the property.

Thus, after the present Queen's accession in 1952, the late John Houison Craufurd approached Her Majesty at Holyrood carrying a silver bowl, flanked by his son (the present laird) and the laird's brother holding a silver jug and a napkin on a tray. Rosewater was then poured from the jug into the bowl for the Queen symbolically to bathe her wounds before drying her fingers on the napkin. All three Houison Craufurds (the present laird then aged nearly seven) also performed the same service for the Queen's father, George VI, in 1937.

The present laird's grandmother, Nellie Houison Craufurd (*née* Dalrymple-Hay), was a colourful Lowland character. The only lady to preside over the Ayrshire Herd Society (her most celebrated bull being Hot Stuff), the redoubtable Nellie turned to education after her family estate of Dunlop had to be sold following an outbreak of foot-and-mouth. She promptly became headmistress of Westonbirt, but is best remembered for running her own school, Downham, in Hertfordshire.

Like his father and uncle the present laird is a member of the Royal Company of Archers (the Queen's Body Guard for Scotland). He was educated at Eton and served in the Scots Guards. In 1965 he married the Honourable Caroline Berry, elder daughter of the 2nd Viscount Kemsley, of the newspaper dynasty, and shortly afterwards they bravely moved

Servitium Lavacri, 1937: John Houison Craufurd (right), his son, Peter, and brother Alexander.

back to Craufurdland Castle which had been let out of the family for some years.

With the help of the architect Pat Lorimer, of Antony Richardson and Partners, and of a grant from the Historic Buildings Council for Scotland, the Houison Craufurds have recently undertaken a restoration of the castle. In effect, they have also divided it in two—they and their three children live in the centre and the east; while the west (with an entrance in the old tower) has been cleverly arranged as a most stylish separate residence, incorporating the former drawing-room and early-19th-century staircase. The old dining-room has been strikingly converted into a bedroom suite complete with spiral staircase and balustrade.

Peter Houison Craufurd farms part of the 600-acre estate at Craufurdland. Some of the shooting is let; there is trout fishing on the Craufurdland Water and coarse fishing in the lake. Over at Braehead, the only remaining property is now let to an hotel but the present laird has no intention of washing his hands of his inheritance from the doughty Jock.

Craufurdland Castle, Kilmarnock, Strathclyde, is open to the public by appointment.

MUNRO OF FOULIS

Above
Captain and Mrs Munro of Foulis.

CLAN associations have become a great force in fostering the Highland spirit around the world and among the most active of the smaller clans are the Munros, whose Mecca is Foulis Castle in Ross-shire, the seat of the Chief, Captain Patrick Munro, 33rd laird of Foulis. At the castle the Chief, who is president of the Clan Association, has set aside a room for Munro memorabilia that forms a living clan museum.

The early history of the Munros is bathed in the traditional Scotch mists of antiquity. Some say they came originally from County Fermanagh in Ireland and received their lands on the northern shore of the Cromarty Firth from Malcolm II in the 11th century. One legend states that the estate was held on the 'whimsical tenure' of providing a bucket of snow to cool the King's wine at Holyrood. Other versions mention snowballs.

Setting aside the snowballs, it seems certain that the Munros were originally vassals of the magnates in those parts, the Earls of Ross. There is no doubt that Robert of Munro was killed in 1369 fighting in defence of William, 5th Earl of Ross, who had already confirmed him in possession of the family lands of 'Estirfowlis' and other properties 'for good and laudable service'.

The old 'gaunt-peaked' castle of Foulis—described as the 'eagle's nest' in a Gaelic poem—is mentioned in a document of 1491 among the Munro papers. Interesting evidence has recently come to light in the shape of the apertures of the coal-hole to the west of the present castle. These have been identified as keyhole gunports of about 1500.

In 1587 'the tower and fortalice' of Foulis is mentioned in another document. Two years later there was—or so the story goes—foul play at Foulis when the Chief, Hector Munro of Foulis, fell ill and decided to avail himself of the services of the loyal witch, Marian McIngarrath. Together they settled on the device of casting his approaching death on to his younger half-brother, George Munro of Obsdale, as a substitute victim.

Marian dug a grave in which the valetudinarian Chief lay down at the midnight hour, lightly sprinkled with green turf garnished with withes. Then the

Above
Foulis: entrance front.

Chief's foster-mother (called Christian, incidentally) departed to consult the neighbouring Devil, returning to tell Miss McIngarrath of her choice—Hector was to live, George to die.

And so it came to pass, George duly handed in his dinner pail in 1590, Hector recovered, brushing off a charge of murder and witchcraft. The obliging Marian was not so fortunate, being strangled and burnt at the stake together with the rest of her coven-fresh harpies.

The wretched George was, however, to have the last laugh from beyond the grave. For in 1651 the Baronetcy of Nova Scotia, created for Hector's son—together with the Chiefship and the Foulis estate— passed to George's grandson following the death of Hector's grandson (the 2nd Baronet) at the age of 16.

In the Jacobite Risings of 1715 and 1745 the Munro Chiefs were on the side of the Hanoverians which spelt trouble for

Foulis Castle. During the old days of clan warfare, a beacon used to be lit on the tower; hence the Munro gathering cry or Gaelic slogan was '*Caisteal Fòlais na theine*' ('Castle Foulis ablaze'). At the end of the 1740s or thereabouts the castle was indeed ablaze once more but this time out of control.

Whether this conflagration was caused by accident or design is not absolutely clear. The tradition is that the Munros' arch-rivals, the Mackenzies, were responsible (one hopes no blame attached to Katharine Mackenzie, a servant at Foulis for 103 years until her death in 1758 aged 117). Certainly the Jacobites had earlier attacked the castle which had been a Hanoverian garrison.

The then Chief, Sir Harry Munro, 7th Baronet (whose father, Sir Robert, the first Colonel of the Black Watch, was killed at Falkirk in 1746), had been captured by the Jacobites at Prestonpans and

Foulis Castle, Ross-shire: west front.

In anticipation of his disputed inheritance, Charles Munro of Culraine (the future 9th Baronet), mortgaged the estate and proceeded to land Foulis in a sorry mess. By the middle of the 19th century the 'princely Seat' was virtually derelict, thanks to the machinations of this disagreeable soldier.

During the last hundred years or so matters have been put right by a succession of much worthier Munro Chiefs. Sir Hector Munro of Foulis, 11th Baronet, an ADC to both Edward VII and George V, was one of the greatest Highlanders of his time, serving as Lord Lieutenant of Ross and Cromarty for a remarkable span of nearly 40 years.

Sir Hector's two sons both died young (the younger being killed in action in the last days of the First World War) and on his own death in 1935 the Baronetcy passed to a male Munro kinsman. Under Sir Hector's will, however, Foulis itself and the Chiefship went to his eldest daughter's eldest son, Patrick Gascoigne, who assumed the style of Munro of Foulis in 1938.

The present Chief, a Deputy Lieutenant and former county councillor for Ross-shire, was taken prisoner with the Seaforth Highlanders on the fall of France in 1940. After the war he married 'Timmie' French from the County Roscommon, a cousin of Lord De Freyne, and, together with the architect Robert Hurd and the help of Historic Buildings Council grants, they have carried out a thorough restoration and redecoration of the castle. Mrs Munro points out that the quaint old kitchen was in use until 1947.

Outside, Mrs Munro, a member of the Council of the National Trust for Scotland, has created a pleasing courtyard garden. The late Sir Iain Moncreiffe of that Ilk described the present Chief as 'one of the most energetic and efficiently modernised farmers in the whole of the Highlands'. Today the 1,300-acre arable estate is farmed in partnership with the Munros' eldest son, Hector, Younger of Foulis. There are two other sons, a daughter and seven grandchildren.

As the Chief says, Foulis is not just his family seat but 'the home of all Munros, Munroes, Monros or Monroes'. The clan has embraced such diverse figures as H. H. Munro ('Saki', the deliciously ironic storyteller) and James Monroe of 'Monroe Doctrine' fame (the 5th president of the United States of America)—if not, alas, the latter's countrywoman, Marilyn of that ilk.

imprisoned at Glamis. With noble humanity Sir Harry held no grudge against the Jacobites and set about rebuilding Foulis Castle on or near its former site.

Foulis has a decidedly Dutch style, which doubtless reflects the Scholar Chief's education at Leyden University, though the lofty four-storey tower (dated 1754) on the west front harks back to an older Scotch tradition. The west front is approached from an impressive castellated courtyard pierced by three archways and surrounded by stables, carriage houses, laundry and bakehouse.

In his *Episcopal Journal* for August 1762 the inveterate sightseer Bishop Forbes noted that Foulis Castle was:

> one of the most delightfully sited places I ever saw, & a mighty fine House ... we went upon the Balcony ... where we had an extensive prospect of Cromarty Bay and a commanding view of a rich Country of Corn Fields.

Sir Harry, 'a most agreeable and entertaining Gentleman', had a 'large library with two globes in it' and some fine pictures, including a 'Michael Angelo'. 'In a word,' the Bishop concluded, 'Foulis Castle is quite Elysian, in a most charming site, decorated with finished Policies and may truly be termed a princely Seat.'

The present pedimented east facade dates from a remodelling later in the 18th century by Sir Harry's son, Sir Hugh, the 8th Baronet, when it became the entrance front. Unfortunately Sir Hugh's wife was drowned while bathing in the Cromarty Firth and their only surviving child, a daughter, was a hunchback.

Foulis Castle, Evanton, Ross-shire, is open by appointment only.

PART II
THE 16th AND 17th CENTURIES

HANHAM OF
DEANS COURT

Deans Court, Dorset: entrance front.

WHAT do the Martock bean, the commander pea and the Baronetcy have in common? The double answer is that they are all endangered species (the venerable vegetables having been removed from the EEC 'Permitted List', while no new additions have been made to the Baronetage since 1964) which happen to flourish at Deans Court in Dorset.

This delightful country house tucked unexpectedly away on the edge of Wimborne Minster, only two minutes' walk from the Minster itself, is the seat of the Hanham Baronets and also the first sanctuary for threatened vegetables.

The house was once the Deanery to the Wimborne Minster College of Canons, founded in 1100. Traces of a medieval structure survived in the atmospheric cellar (which was used as a location in the television serial *Moonfleet*) and the tradition is that there was once a secret passage from the Deanery to the Minster. At the Dissolution of the Chantries in 1548, the College of Secular Canons was closed down, the Minster Church became a 'Royal Peculiar' and the lease of the Deanery and its manors was granted to John Hanham, the MP for Poole.

Opposite
Deans Court: east and north fronts.

Deans Court: inner hall.

The Hanhams, originally Somerset yeomen, had advanced themselves into the squirearchy through the marriage in about 1487 of John's grandfather to the Long heiress of Purse Caundle in Dorset. John would appear to have been playing an active part in the dispersal of church lands; presumably he decided to grab this prime site, combining the benefits of town and country, for himself.

His son, Thomas Hanham, Serjeant-at-Law, the son-in-law of Lord Chief Justice Popham, bought the freehold towards the end of the 16th century. Four hundred years later it remains the property of the Hanham family.

The Baronetcy was created in 1667 for William Hanham (the Serjeant's great-grandson), a substantial landowner who suffered financially at the hands of his domineering wife, Elizabeth Cooper, a staunchly Catholic niece of the 1st Earl of Shaftesbury, the statesman seated at Wimborne St Giles. Playfair's *Baronetage* records how this lady alienated several estates and, as a widow, kept her minor son out of all profits until he was 25.

In 1674, three years after her unfortunate husband's death, an Act of Parliament had to be passed to pay the late Baronet's debts (including the unsettled down payment for his very title) out of his real property. By way of poetic justice the extravagant Elizabeth ended her days in prison, the only woman among the adherents (including Judge Jeffreys) of James II to be committed by William and Mary to the Tower of London.

The family fortunes were recouped by her son, Sir John Hanham, 2nd Baronet. He had the sense to marry the Eyre heiress from Wiltshire whose saintly disposition earned her the description of 'an incomparable lady'. It was their son, Sir William Hanham, 3rd Baronet, who was responsible for the elegant 18th-century house we see today.

In 1725 the 3rd Baronet greatly enlarged the old deanery (which came to be known as Deans Court), giving it a stylish dark-red brick facade, adorned with stone pilasters and a balustrade. Over the entrance on the north front is a pediment with the Hanham arms.

Inside, the large panelled hall in the centre of the house recalls the proportions of the earlier building. The early 18th-century cantilevered stone staircase is approached through the attractive screen in the hall. The dentil cornice in the morning room is reminiscent of one at Smedmore in the same county; this leads the Hanhams to wonder whether the Bastard dynasty of Dorset architects and joinery may have had a hand in the improvements to Deans Court.

The black sheep of the Hanham family was the wild Sir William Thomas Hanham, 5th Baronet, who drank himself to death in 1791. He is referred to as 'the spendthrift cousin' in the family memoir, *A Leading Case* (1904), which tells how the Lesters of Poole continually frustrated the romance between Sarah Pointer (*née* Lester) and the Reverend Sir James Hanham, 7th Baronet. Sarah seems ultimately to have exacerbated her family's opposition to the match by rubbing it in to the wife of her brother, a mere knight, that, as a Baronet's lady, she would take precedence.

The feud between the Lesters and the Hanhams was later healed by the marriage of Sarah's great-niece, Amy (author of *A Leading Case*), to the 7th Baronet's youngest son, Captain John Hanham. Following the Captain's murder at Preston in 1861 Amy married one of the estate trustees, Judge Caillard.

In 1868, before her remarriage, Amy Caillard carried out the third significant stage of Deans Court's building history. This entailed the rebuilding of the south, or rear, of the house, with an extra storey, in a 'Tudor-Gothic' style to the designs of M. Davis of Langport. The kitchen (now the herb garden) was demolished and rehoused in the room previously used for the manorial court. The curtains in the drawing-room are the handiwork of Amy, a noted needlewoman.

Her son, John Hanham, a barrister, succeeded to the Baronetcy in 1877 but could not afford to live at Deans Court until his marriage to the Honourable Cordelia Lopes nearly 20 years later. After Sir John's death in 1911, time rather stood still at the Court—electricity was finally installed in the 1930s.

Cordelia remained there with her three unmarried children until her death in 1945. The latter years of the younger son, Sir Henry Hanham, 11th Baronet, a dedicated ornithologist, gardener and crack shot were somewhat overshadowed by the threat of a bypass cutting through the estate.

Upon his death in 1973, Sir Henry was succeeded in the Baronetcy and at Deans Court by his cousin Michael, who had won the DFC with the 'Pathfinders' of Bomber Command in the Second World War. Keen on carpentry since his school days at Winchester, Sir Michael formerly

ran his own garden furniture workshop in Kent where he met his wife, Jane (*née* Thomas). They have a son, William, who is with Christie's, and a daughter, Victoria, a decorator.

The baking summer of 1976 caused the roof lead to crack and because of the resulting leaks the Hanhams last year had to undertake a major rebuilding of the roof. A 40 per cent grant was forthcoming from the Historic Buildings and Monu-

Sir Michael and Lady Hanham.

ments Commission and, as a consequence, Deans Court is open to the public by written appointment.

The 13 acres of gardens, however, are open regularly. Despite their proximity to the town, the partly wild gardens contain a remarkable variety of wildlife. The River Allen (formerly the Wim) runs picturesquely through the park feeding the old monastery fish pond. The interesting specimen trees include two believed to have been brought back by Thomas Hanham from an exploration of the Americas in 1606—the tulip tree and the Mexican swamp cypress, thought to be the tallest example in this country.

The walled kitchen garden (now, alas, overlooked by most unsympathetic new buildings) has a lengthy serpentine wall, over a quarter of a mile of box hedge and good organic soil vouched for by the Soil Association. Here the Hanhams grow several varieties of threatened vegetables in connection with the Henry Doubleday Research Association. 'Most of them seem to us to compare favourably for taste with later varieties,' Lady Hanham says. I can vouch for this, having enjoyed an excellent lunch with the Hanhams. Lady H's wholefood teas are one of the highlights of a visit to this enchanting family seat.

Deans Court, Wimborne Minster, Dorset, is open by written appointment but the gardens are open regularly (as advertised).

PUXLEY OF WELFORD

Major and Mrs John Puxley with their elder son, James.

F OR some people Berkshire conjures up images of bijoux villas near Maidenhead and the 'various bogus Tudor bars' thereabouts pilloried in Sir John Betjeman's hymn of hate on *Slough*. West of Reading, however, the other Berkshire (celebrated in several more of the lamented Poet Laureate's poems, such as *Upper Lambourn* and *Indoor Games near Newbury*) remains reassuringly rural.

Until recently it was said to be possible to walk from Newbury to Wantage, traversing the land of only four families. Happily, the Loyds are still at Lockinge and the Wroughtons at Woolley and the Puxleys are seated at Welford, an estate that has passed by a complex inheritance since 1618.

In that year the old monastic site and sometime royal hunting lodge was bought from the Parry family by Sir Francis Jones, a well-to-do merchant soon to be Lord Mayor of London. Later in the 17th century, about 1680, the sole Jones heiress, Mary, married John Archer, whose family owned land in Essex. It was they who are thought to have been responsible for the remodelling of the house at the beginning of the 18th century. This resulted in the refacing of the red-brick façade and the adornment with stone dressings including a pediment and giant pilasters.

The hipped roof and 'extremely curious brick details' (some of the brick is in Flemish 'bond', some in English) led Sir Nikolaus Pevsner in his *Berkshire* volume to comment that Welford seemed to date from something like 1660–70. The windows (those on the ground floor regrettably lost their glazing bars in the 19th century), have remarkable raised frames vertically connected by a raised band standing on the centre of each lower window. Pevsner placed Welford in the school of provincial classicism dubbed 'Artisan Mannerism' by Sir John Summerson.

There is, however, an intriguing connection between Welford and a great architect who was far from a provincial artisan—Thomas Archer, best known for his north front at Chatsworth. Though no apparent relation to John Archer, the architect did happen to marry his only child, Eleanor (who died of smallpox within a year, in 1702).

The family tradition is therefore that Thomas Archer advised his parents-in-law on the remodelling of the house. Architecturally, the exterior seems rather too restrained for such a master of the Baroque, but there is perhaps a hint of Archer's grandiosity in the hall screens inside. In any event, what we see today is a most lovable tall 'doll's house'.

After John Archer's death in 1706 Welford passed to his niece, Eleanora Wrottesley, a member of the long-established Staffordshire dynasty of that name, who married William Eyre (later Archer). There were no children of the marriage (Eleanora died in 1720) and all the subsequent owners of Welford descend from William's second marriage. His bride was Susanna Newton, daughter of Sir John Newton, 3rd Baronet, of Culverthorpe in Lincolnshire, a neighbour, friend and indeed (as it was conveniently proved) a distant cousin of the great Sir Isaac.

Susanna turned out to be a considerable heiress, eventually inheriting the Culverthorpe estate in 1743 upon the death of here brother, Sir Michael Newton, 4th Baronet, who is depicted with his hounds in the large Wootton painting in the handsome panelled staircase hall at Welford. Sir Michael's direct heir, an infant son, had apparently had the misfortune of being thrown out of a top-floor window by a pet monkey (a sorry contrast to the ape who is supposed to have rescued the young FitzGerald heir from a fire in Ireland some five centuries before).

In 1770 the family came into another

Opposite
Welford Park, Berkshire: entrance front.

estate when Susanna's grand-daughter and namesake married Jacob Houblon of Hallingbury Place in Essex. The autumn wedding at Welford is delightfully recorded in Parson Abdy's diary. The vicar from Hallinbury describes how 'Mr Archer and Mr Houblon went forth with their dogs and guns threatening amazing destruction to the Partridges', and their other sporting excursion 'to some river at no great distance with the full intention of bringing home an enormous pike or two'.

The Houblons, a distinguished Huguenot family, also feature in a better-known diary—that of Samuel Pepys, who was an intimate friend of Sir John Houblon, first Governor of the Bank of England.

Culverthorpe and Hallingbury remained in the Archer-Houblon family until the 1920s and Welford became a subsidiary seat. But in 1831 a younger son, Charles Archer-Houblon (who changed his name to Eyre) came to live at Welford and embarked on a series of improvements. These were to include the diversion of the Newbury-Lambourn road; the insertion of a bow-fronted dining-room in between the projecting wings at the back of the house; the rebuilding of the church (to the designs of T. Talbot Bury), and the erection of the stables. The gory Eyre crest (a severed leg which traditionally proved useful to an ancestor in battle) was placed atop the front entrance gates.

In the 1950s Charles's grandson, Major Henry Archer-Houblon (whose father resumed this surname), a bachelor squire dedicated to the pursuit of game both big and small, decided to leave the estate to his niece, Aline (née Wilson), the wife of Major John Puxley. She attributes her inheritance to her uncle's liking for her husband, a sound shooting man.

Major Puxley, who served in the Second World War with the Berkshire Yeomanry and later became a solicitor, was High Sheriff of the county in 1970. He comes from a family that has owned land in Ireland (their Dunboy Castle near the Puxley copper mines in County Cork was burnt in 1921) and Wales. The still extant Welsh estate at Llethr Llestri in the old county of Carmarthenshire is to pass to the Puxleys' younger son, Charles, a former Captain in the Green Jackets.

The Welford estate of nearly 3,000 acres is run by the Puxley's elder son, James, a chartered surveyor. Most of the land is farmed in hand and James Puxley, an enthusiastic forester, is carrying out an extensive replanting scheme on the 600 acres of woodland. Welford is still engagingly feudal. In the best traditions there is also a cricket ground in the park where I have had the pleasure of playing a few times.

Welford Park, near Newbury, Berkshire, is not open to the public, though the gardens are generally opened in February, for the snowdrops.

Opposite
Welford: staircase.

GRAHAM OF NORTON CONYERS

Above
Norton Conyers, Yorkshire: stables.

IN 1839, during a disagreeable stint as governess to the 'riotous, perverse, unmanageable cubs' of the Sidgwick family, Charlotte Brontë visited Norton Conyers, the seat of the Graham Baronets which was then tenanted by Mrs Sidgwick's parents, the Greenwoods. According to Charlotte's closest friend, Ellen Nussey, Miss Brontë was much impressed by the story she heard there about the Graham family legend of the 'Mad Woman'.

Sometime in the 18th century an unhinged female is supposed to have been confined in the remotest corner of the attics at Norton Conyers, a room still known as the 'Mad Woman's Room'. No doubt this gave Charlotte the idea for the crazed Mrs Rochester in *Jane Eyre*.

It also seems more than likely that Norton Conyers was one of the models on which she drew for 'Thornfield Hall', ill-fated seat of that sardonic squire, Mr Rochester. Certainly there are striking similarities between Thornfield and Norton Conyers, such as the broad oak staircase lit by a high, latticed window, and the high square hall covered in family portraits.

Two of the largest portraits in the hall feature the squire of Norton Conyers at the time of Miss Brontë's visit, Sir Bellingham Graham, 7th Bt, a colourful sportsman who was sometime Master of the Badsworth, Atherstone, Pytchley, Hambledon, Quorn, Albrighton and Shropshire Hunts.

Having inherited the baronetcy as a child in 1796, the wild young Sir Bellingham indulged himself to the full. Apart from his lavish hunting exploits, he had a string of racehorses and won the St Leger in 1816 with his mare 'Duchess'. According to Jeremy Graham, formerly Master of the Bedale and uncle of the present Baronet, Sir Bellingham's coffers were extended still further by having to maintain the unlikely geographical combination of a French mistress at Norton

Above
Norton Conyers: entrance front.

Conyers and an English wife in Paris.

One of the portraits is a sizeable Beechey of 1813 showing Sir Bellingham as a dashing young officer of Hussars. The other, a vast canvas depicting the Quorn Hunt in 1822, was painted by John Ferneley; Sir Bellingham is mounted on the Baron, the bay horse beneath the lefthand limb of the tree. On the picture's completion the sisters met to throw dice for it, but Sir Bellingham was unable to be there and asked a friend to throw for him. The friend threw double six; thus the picture ended up at Norton Conyers.

By the time of Sir Bellingham's death in 1866, the family fortunes squandered on his sport, Norton Conyers and many of its contents had had to be sold. This could have been the end of the Grahams' connection with the historic manor house but fortunately Sir Reginald Graham, whose Shiffner wife was a considerable heiress, managed to buy the place back in the 1880s. A hundred years on, Norton Conyers remains the seat of his great-grandson Sir James Graham, 11th Bt, an historical archivist, with an estate of about 1,400 acres (let to four tenant farmers).

In Norman times the estate was part of the Conyers family's extensive land-holdings in the north. This portion passed by marriage into the Norton family in the mid-14th century; hence the name, Norton Conyers. In 1569 the Nortons took part in the Catholic 'Rising of the North' against Elizabeth I and consequently forfeited their ownership to the Crown. The next owners were the Musgraves, one of whom married Richard Graham, from a turbulent Border family with a reputation for cattle stealing.

Graham, a connoisseur of horse-flesh, first made his mark as Gentleman of the Horse to James I's favourite, the Duke of Buckingham. In 1623 he so impressed James I by the swiftness of his return with despatches from Spain that the punster-King added a pair of wings to the Graham coat of arms. The following year Graham bought Norton Conyers from his father-in-law, Sir Thomas Musgrave, and later bought another property, Netherby in Cumberland.

Following the egregious Buckingham's assassination in 1628, Richard Graham became Gentleman of the Horse to Charles I, who created him a Baronet. A loyal Cavalier, Sir Richard fought in the Civil War; the story goes that after he had been wounded at Marston Moor in 1644, his horse galloped him all the way home to Norton Conyers, in through the front door and across the hall. The game steed is then supposed to have placed one of its hot iron shoes on the bottom step. The alleged hoof print, later removed to another part of the staircase, can still be seen, though spoilsports think it is just a knot in the wood.

The principal staircase had been installed a dozen years before Marston Moor, at the same time as the Dutch gables were added to the exterior. The basic structure of the present house dates from the late 15th century when the Nortons were here; it was formerly a plain, red-brick semi-fortified manor house (the rough-cast is a much later addition). Traces of the battlements and the one surviving arrow-slit can be seen from the Bowling Green.

After Sir Richard Graham's death in 1654, his Netherby property and the baronetcy passed to his elder son, George; while Norton Conyers went to his younger son, also called Richard, who was created a Baronet in his own right in 1662. A portrait to the left of the fireplace in the hall shows young Richard holding a coral teething rattle.

As a boy he gave a vivid description of a day's coursing in a letter (among the Norton Conyers muniments) addressed to 'Dear Daddy', describing how his 'dog Juniper toke [the hare] by ye buttocks' and looking forward to having 'so excellent a straine of hounds as any in England fitting for to run before a King'. In 1679 he entertained a future king, James II, at Norton Conyers when the then Duke and Duchess of York spent a night here; the bed they 'lay' in still adorns 'King James's Room'.

The late-18th century remodelling of Norton Conyers was carried out by the page's grandson, Sir Bellingham Graham, 5th Bt, the painting of whose family (supposedly by Zoffany) is in the parlour. Most of the new features were designed by William Belwood, a local architect who had been associated with Robert Adam at Newby. He was responsible for the chimney-piece (£63.6s.7d. in 1781) in the

Norton Conyers: hall.

Norton Conyers: chimneypiece in dining-room.

parlour; the plasterwork and bow windows in both that room and the dining-room; and also the handsome stable yard. The classical dining-room has portraits by Romney of the 6th Baronet and his wife, as well as the luscious Batoni over the chimneypiece of another passionate sportsman, Sir Humphrey Morice (no apparent relation), who left £600 a year to keep his hounds and horses after his death.

Undaunted by the 7th Baronet's crashing financial fall, the Grahams continued to enjoy their sport. The extravagant Sir Bellingham's son and successor, Sir Reginald Graham, 8th Bt, was a dedicated rider to hounds and published his *Foxhunting Recollections* in 1908; the 9th Baronet, Sir Guy, hunted the Hurworth, while his brother, Malise, one of the most brilliant equestrians of his day, won the King's Cup at Olympia on his great horse, Broncho, before breaking his neck at the

Dublin Horse Show in 1929. The present Baronet's father, Sir Richard Graham, 10th Bt, also loved joining his brother, Jeremy, out with the Bedale which meets at Norton Conyers. A banker by training, the late Sir Richard was the first chairman of Yorkshire Television. He served as High Sheriff of the county in 1961.

His widow, the former Beatrice Spencer-Smith, takes a particular interest in the Norton Conyers nursery. Set in the agreeable two-acre 18th-century walled garden, this specialises in unusual hardy plants and is open all the year. The Orangery (of about 1776) has recently been restored. Other features of the gardens include early 18th-century lead statues of Mars, Apollo and Diana. Despite the changes made since the family's purchase in 1624, the atmosphere of this seat of the galloping Grahams remains essentially Jacobean—inspiration indeed for a certain Miss Brontë.

Norton Conyers: chimneypiece in dining-room.

Norton Conyers, near Ripon, North Yorkshire, is open as advertised in the summer. The garden centre is open all year (Monday to Friday).

JEFFREYS OF NEWHOUSE

Newhouse, Wiltshire: rear entrance.

FOUR hundred years ago, in 1586, Geoffrey Whitney defined the newly fashionable 'devices' as 'something obscure to be perceived at the first, whereby when with further consideration it is understood, it may the greater delight the beholder'. In late-Tudor and Jacobean architecture these devices were to take the form of circles, triangles, Greek crosses, letters of the alphabet ('E' for Elizabeth) and so forth. Of the houses built in the shape of a 'Y' (supposed to represent a monogram of the Trinity), only two are thought to survive. Both, oddly enough, are called Newhouse— one is a farm near Goodrich in Herefordshire, the other is the seat of The Jeffreys family in Wiltshire.

Tradition has it that Newhouse was designed by the architect John Thorpe (1570–1610), who had a penchant for curious devices. He is known to have had a hand in the triangular Longford Castle nearby. Longford was owned by the Gorges family and Newhouse has been said to have been built as their hunting lodge.

According to Sir Richard Colt Hoare's *History of Modern Wiltshire* (1844), however, the property on which Newhouse stands, then called Tychebourne, was not conveyed to Sir Edward Gorges, 1st Baronet, until 1619 by one William Stockman. In the indenture of that year there is a reference to a 'Mansion ... late erected within the scyte of the pales of the park'.

Opposite
Newhouse: main entrance.

Above
Detail of 'Hare' picture at Newhouse.

Right
Mr and Mrs George Jeffreys.

Thus, it is not clear whether the house was built by the Stockmans or by the Gorges family on the Stockman's land.

Sir Edward Gorges, who received an Irish peerage the year after the acquisition of Newhouse, was the son of the Eliza-bethan courtier Sir Thomas Gorges, the man who arrested Mary Queen of Scots in 1586. Sir Edward (or rather the 1st Lord Gorges of Dundalk) overreached himself in the unsuccessful project to drain the fens of Lincolnshire and sold up the Longford estate. The castle was sold to the Hares who, in turn, eventually sold it to the ancestor of the present owner, the Earl of Radnor.

Newhouse was conveyed in 1633 to Giles Eyre who lived at Brickworth nearby and was a prominent Cromwellian. It has remained in this family ever since. The present owner, George Jeffreys, took over the estate from his late uncle, John Eyre-Matcham in the 1970s.

On his father's side, Mr Jeffreys is related to the much-maligned 'Judge' Jeffreys. The notorious punisher of the 1685 'Pitchfork' rebels is not the only Lord Chief Justice in the family for Sir Robert Eyre, once described as 'one of the truly foremost men in England', was appointed Lord Chief Justice of the Common Pleas in 1725.

Sir Robert's father, Sir Samuel Eyre, also a judge, had bought Newhouse for £2,000 at the time of the Restoration from his erstwhile Cromwellian cousin, William Eyre, MP. Sir Robert, born, presumably at Newhouse, in 1666, was appointed Solicitor-General in 1707. Through his influence Queen Anne granted the port of Bristol a new charter, specifying that he should be its first Alderman and Recorder. (He had already done stints as Recorder of Salisbury and Southampton.) Under George I he became Chancellor to the Prince of Wales (later George II).

Sir Robert certainly looks a formidable character in his likenesses at Newhouse. The marble bust in the dining-room confirms Alexander Pope's observation that the end of the world would come before a smile from Lord Chief Justice Eyre.

Following the death of the Lord Chief Justice in 1735, his son Robert Eyre, MP, a trustee of the new American colony of Georgia, embarked on a series of improvements to Newhouse. These included the installation of a new staircase and the addition of a north-west wing (downpipes dated 1742), to the left of the central block. The south-east wing (containing a drawing-room fit to entertain the Mayor and Corporation of Salisbury) was added in about 1760 by Robert's cousin and successor, Samuel Eyre, MP.

'Bad Sam', as he is known in the family, was an extravagant squire who sold many of the contents of Newhouse but ended up as a clergyman in Exmouth. The estate passed to his daughter, Susannah, who put up an elaborate Gothic porch.

Susannah's daughter, Harriet, married a nephew of the great Horatio Nelson, George Matcham. An antiquarian, Matcham assisted Sir Richard Colt Hoare on his *Modern History of Wiltshire* and installed the panelling in the dining-room at Newhouse from Downton Church. Of his son, William Eyre-Matcham, a Deputy Lieutenant and Justice of the Peace, a fellow rhymester wrote:

. . . there lives a bard
His hat is flat
His' name is Matcham
He makes up verses by the yard
I can't think how his brain can hatch 'em.

'Flat Hat' added a cumbrous service wing to Newhouse in 1879. His son, George, an enthusiastic rider to hounds, married Constance Glyn of the banking family. When they came into Newhouse in 1906 they removed the Gothic porch and added a bow window to the drawing-room which was itself tricked up in the Carolean style by Maples.

This fine Edwardian interior has recently been stylishly restored by June Jeffreys, the wife of the present owner, in a cameo colour. The 19th-century classical ceiling in the dining-room has also been restored. The library still has its orginal early 17th-century fireplace.

In the early 1970s Newhouse was, as Mr and Mrs Jeffreys recall, 'virtually derelict'. There was a hole from the roof to the ground floor, only one lavatory and no electricity (an acetylene gas plant provided light up to the late 1960s). With the help of Historic Buildings Council grants and the architect Kenneth Wiltshire, Mr and Mrs Jeffreys set about a five-year rescue operation of the Grade I-listed house. The Victorian service wing, riddled with dry rot, was pulled down and the rest of the house was completely refloored.

Born in 1931, George Jeffreys was educated at Radley and Cirencester. Before farming in Wiltshire, he worked as a jackaroo in Australia, an overland bus driver to Bombay and a cattle-rancher in Kenya. He married June Bennett, an enthusiastic student of costume, in 1960 and they have three daughters.

The 1,300-acre Newhouse estate on the edge of Salisbury includes 650 acres of woodlands and a 450-acre dairy enterprise

Aerial view of the 'Y'-shaped Newhouse.

which Mr Jeffreys farms in partnership. As many Wiltshire people will testify, the Pensworth Farm Dairy on the estate produces delicious cream and milk. The shooting is let to a syndicate, though the deer stalking on the estate is reserved.

Among the attractions at Newhouse, which has been open regularly to the public for the last dozen years, is a jolly assortment of old agricultural and domestic implements set around the atmospheric outbuildings. Inside the delightfully engaging old manor house visitors can see Mrs Jeffrey's costume collection and several items of 'Nelsoniana' such as young Horatio's cot (probably made by a ship's carpenter). This natural daughter of the Admiral's by Emma Hamilton was largely brought up by Catherine Matcham (George's mother) whose portrait is above the chimney-piece in the drawing-room.

The most extraordinary object on view at Newhouse is the 'Hare' picture, said to have been painted about 1640 as a satirical attack on the contemporary Court party. With its luridly detailed depiction of a trip of hares hunting, teasing, killing and feasting upon humans, the canvas provides uncomfortable food for thought for field sportsmen.

Newhouse, Redlynch, Wiltshire, is open to the public in the summer months (as advertised).

BLOFELD OF HOVETON

Mr and Mrs Thomas Blofeld.

I N the 16th and 17th centuries the heralds went on an historically important series of visitations round the country in order to record the pedigrees and coats of arms of the local gentry. Today there are few 'visitation families' surviving in the male line who still own landed estates. However, the fertile agricultural county of Norfolk, still something of a world apart, can claim a comparatively respectable total of ten survivors (plus another eight descended through the female line) and among them are the Blofelds of Hoveton St John. Their late-17th-century family seat, Hoveton House, is open (by written appointment only) to interested groups.

The Blofelds, who have mainly been 'squarsons' and lawyers, acquired armorial bearings at the end of the 16th century when Thomas Blofeld (let us call him, for clarity's sake, 'Tom the Second') of Sustead Hall was called to the Bar. His mother—the wife of Tom the First—was a Doughty of Hanworth and it happened to be from another branch of the Doughtys that the Blofelds bought the manor of Hoveton St John in 1667.

The exquisitely pretty gardener's cottage in the grounds, known as Greengates, dates from the Doughtys' time—as evidenced by their coat of arms above the door. Hoveton's purchaser, Tom the

Opposite
Hoveton House, Norfolk: south front.

Hoveton: dining-room

time around 1680. As Michael Sayer has pointed out, Hoveton is an intimate example of the classicism catching on in the county at the time.

The red brick facade on the south front is engagingly set off by stone dressings, including giant Corinthian pilasters and a steep pediment. The central ground-floor window (originally the front door) has a pediment with the arms of Blofeld impaling Negus and what Sir Nikolaus Pevsner calls 'not very disciplined' foliar carving.

The previous house on the site—a much smaller structure—was incorporated in the building. This accounts for the irregularity of the gabled north front which became the entrance front at the beginning of this century. Interior features of architectural note include the staircase (with two twisted balusters to each tread); an original late-17th-century plaster ceiling in a bedroom alcove; and, above all, the Georgian decorative carving in the principal rooms.

The overmantel in the present drawing-room (formerly the dining-room) and the fireplace, overmantel and overdoor in the present dining-room (made up of two smaller rooms thrown into one) are all in the style of Thomas Ivory, the Norwich architect and builder known to have been an acquaintance of the Blofelds.

These Georgian embellishments were carried out by Tom the Fourth's daughter and heiress, Sarah, who married her cousin John Blofeld in 1753—a convenient match ensuring the male line survival of the Blofelds of Hoveton. More radical changes were contemplated by their son, Tom the Fifth, chairman of the Norfolk Quarter Sessions, when he inherited the property in 1805.

Two years later, Humphry Repton, the great East Anglian landscapist who could seldom resit proposing architectural alterations, produced a scheme to transform Hoveton into an Italianate villa, with a pedimented gable and balustraded balcony. On his sketch plan Repton scrawled: 'When the house is brought to one Colour by a Wash the carving enrichment of the Stone pilasters will be very little seen but they may be chopped off if you disapprove them.'

Fortunately, Tom the Fifth and his wife decided against any such white-washing or chopping off, merely taking Repton's advice as to the installation of a ha-ha and the planting of radiating spokes of trees in the park. Repton does not seem to have been put out and wrote a friendly letter suggesting that Mrs Blofeld should make

Second's grandson, Tom the Third, had gradually been putting together an estate in these parts.

In partnership with his brother-in-law, Henry Negus of Hoveton St Peter, he made a fortune 'in buying, selling and uttering of all manner of hose shortings'. These 'shortings', apparently some sort of undergarment to be worn under breeches (shades of P. G. Wodehouse's character Roderick Spode, *alias* Lord Sidcup, whose cash came from ladies' lingerie) proved particularly popular in the Iberian Peninsula.

Tom the Third went on to become MP for Norwich, Mayor of the City, and a Deputy Lieutenant and Justice of the Peace for the county, dying a childless widower in 1708. In his will he bequeathed the Hoveton estate to his great-nephew, Tom the Fourth, whose mother came from a prominent Norfolk dynasty, the Calthorpes of Hickling. Also included in the bequest was a brick-kiln—presumably the source for the lovely red bricks used in the building of Hoveton House some years earlier.

There is no record of exactly when the present house was built by Tom the Third, but it is thought to have been some

two little fans for her chimneypiece out of his 'before' and 'after' drawings. One cannot help noticing that Repton's 'before' version of Hoveton distorts the charm of the house.

It would appear that Tom the Fifth, who died in 1817, landed the estate in a financial tangle. His successors, Tom the Sixth and Tom the Seventh, both 'squarsons', certainly had a difficult inheritance to maintain. Matters were put to rights at the end of the 19th century by Tom the Eighth, a barrister and sound business-man who was Chancellor of the Diocese of Norwich and chairman of the Norwich Union.

In 1920 Tom the Eighth's son and successor, John, died suddenly of anthrax which he had caught from a cow, leaving his son, Tom the Ninth, then aged 17 and hoping to become a doctor, as the squire of Hoveton. Young Tom had to change his plans and devote himself to agriculture. More than 65 years later, this much-loved Norfolk figure—possessor of an unmis-takable profile and, despite his black eye patch, the very antithesis of the villain for whom Ian Fleming 'borrowed' his surname—is still happily *in situ* at Hoveton, together with his artistic wife, Grizel (*née* Turner, of Yarmouth de-scent), the historian of the family.

Those years have seen a sympathetic renovation and enhancement of the house and estate. The number of men employed, including those in the enchanting garden, has decreased from 40 (plus 40 horses) to nine. Today the acreage is about 1,200, made up of 700 acres of upland farmed in hand (corn, peas, sugar-beet, potatoes and fruit) and the rest woodland, marsh and two broads (stuffed with pike). There is a nature trail on the estate run in conjunc-tion with the Nature Conservancy Council.

The present squire was High Sheriff of the county in 1953 and became a magis-trate the following year. Until 1971, he was chairman of the Country Gentle-men's Assocation, being succeeded by his son John, now a circuit judge. The Blo-felds' daughter, Anthea Salmon, is a psy-chiatric consultant and their younger son, Henry, is the well-known cricket-writer and mellifluous broadcaster who first played cricket for Norfolk while a legend-ary prodigy at Eton and, despite a bad motor accident, went on to gain a Blue at Cambridge. Visitors to Hoveton who find themselves being shown round by 'Blowers' can be sure of a good earful.

In the best squirearchical traditions, the Blofelds of Hoveton have husbanded their land (Tom the Fourth once wrote that 'heavenly tillage was my glorious care'), looked after their house and village and taken their part in local public affairs. And the story will surely continue. Tom the Tenth, Judge Blofeld's elder son, recently celebrated his coming of age.

Hoveton House, Wroxham, Norfolk, is open to the public by written appointment.

Hoveton: Greengates, the gardener's cottage in grounds.

MILBANK OF BARNINGHAM

Portrait of Lady Augusta Milbank in the dining-room at Barningham Park, North Yorkshire.

AMONG the papers of the Milbank family, which acquired the Barningham estate near the 'Richmondshire' bank of the River Tees some 300 years ago, is a manuscript copy of the Bedale Hunt Song. The penultimate verse goes:

> Here's a bumper to Milbank, the source
> of our sport
> A bumper to him, and his hounds Sir,
> *Brim full it* shall *be* of the finest old port
> Where health and good humour
> abounds Sir.

The Milbank referred to in this jolly toast is the Hunt's founder (and Master for 24 seasons), Mark Milbank, who is portrayed in the centre of Anson Martin's vast canvas of the Bedale Field in 1840 that hangs above the staircase at Barningham.

Barningham itself is in Zetland rather than Bedale country. The estate straddles the border of the old North Riding of Yorkshire and County Durham; indeed, on the estate cricket pitch, one bowler delivers from Yorkshire, the other from Durham.

In the 18th and 19th centuries the Milbanks made their home principally at Thorp Perrow in the heart of the Bedale country [see PART IV]. Barningham was then used as a secondary residence or shooting-box.

Nonetheless, Mark Milbank and his wife, Lady Augusta Vane, daughter of the Durham magnate the 2nd Duke of Cleveland, decided that certain improvements were necessary at Barningham and duly added ungainly Victorian service wings to the north. These have recently been nipped off as part of a general renovation of Barningham undertaken with the advice of the distinguished present-day Georgian architect, Francis Johnson.

In origin, the Milbanks (or Milbankes) seem to have derived from the vicinity of Barningham in the 13th century. They later migrated to Newcastle-upon-Tyne where, in the 17th century, an earlier

Above
Barningham: cast front.

Mark Milbanke became a prominent merchant adventurer and consolidated the family fortunes by marrying one of the four co-heiresses of the immensely rich Mayor, Ralph Cock. The great expectations of these girls gave rise to a local adage—'as rich as Cock's canny hinnies'.

By the end of the 17th century the family had advanced to a baronetcy and the ownership of seats at Halnaby, Thorp Perrow and Barningham. The baronetcy (created for Mark Milbanke's son in recognition of his father's generosity to the exiled Charles II) descended down the senior line of the Milbanke family until its dormancy in 1949.

The 6th Baronet's only child, Annabella, was married briefly—and disastrously—to Lord Byron; she left the poet after a year with recriminatory accusations of insanity. Halnaby Hall, the seat of the senior line, noted for its plasterwork, was demolished in 1952.

Barningham was bought shortly before 1690 by Acclom Milbanke, a younger brother of the 2nd Baronet of Halnaby, and later passed by inheritance to the Thorp Perrow branch of the family descended from his brother, John Milbank, who dropped the final 'e' from their surname.

Previously Barningham had been owned by the Barninghams, Scropes and latterly the Tunstalls, descendants of the illustrious Scargills of Scargill Castle nearby. (Speculative attempts have been

Right
Six generations of Milbanks (from left): Sir Powlett, 2nd Bt; Sir Frederick, 3rd Bt; Sir Frederick, 1st Bt; Sir Anthony, 5th Bt; his son, Edward; and Sir Mark, 4th Bt.

made to link Arthur of that ilk to this ancient dynasty.)

Domesday Book records that the mighty Tor had a pre-Conquest hall at Barningham and it would be romantic to think, as Olwen Hedley put it in her enjoyable account of *The Milbank Family* (privately printed) that he 'lived in this same green, secluded spot under the hill and drank of the spring water that cascades into the garden today'. Evidence in

the east wing of Barningham confirms that there was a Tudor or even a medieval house on the site.

As Sir Nikolaus Pevsner observes in his *North Riding* volume, the present structure looks 17th-century in manner. The rusticated doorway on the pleasant principal east front reminds Francis Johnson of the style of the Northumberland architect Robert Trollop. However, a time lag in the diffusion of architectural fashions in

Below
Barningham: drawing-room.

these parts makes any precise dating difficult.

It seems probable that the building work was begun by Acclom Milbanke in the 1690s and then various alterations and improvements (such as the delightfully curious double Venetian windows on the south face of the east wing) followed in the course of the 18th century.

Inside a considerable amount of refurbishment was carried out in the 1790s for William Milbank, the heir of Mark Milbank of Thorp Perrow and Barningham ('killed by a ffall from a Hay Stack in Harvest Time', 1775). This seems to have included the installation of the present main staircase and of the joinery, plaster cornices and chimneypieces in the principal interiors.

William was the father of the founder of the Bedale Hunt, whose own son, Frederick, MP for North Yorkshire, was created a Baronet in 1882. The 1st Baronet 'Fred the Rip', was a celebrated Gun. He once accounted for 190 grouse in a single drive lasting 20 minutes. Although the Rip confined his own sport to game, his remarkable Victorian *Game Book* was printed to embrace everything from otters to a golden eagle.

The bag of the Rip's reckless elder son, Harry, a notorious duellist on the Continent, was more bizarre. His tally of unsuccessful opponents slain in a series of picaresque adventures across Poland, Germany and France included a brace-and-a-half from the same countly family. Sadly, this colourful character—always ready to defend a lady's honour and legendary for his lavish garden parties at Barningham—drifted into drug addiction in Paris, and died in Switzerland in 1892.

Ten years later the duellist's brother, Sir Powlett Milbank, 2nd Baronet, sold Thorp Perrow and Barningham became the principal seat of this branch of the family. The pair of photographs (illustrated here) charmingly show the succession to the baronetcy, featuring the six generations down to the present day. The sporting reputation of the family is currently upheld by the Chantilly trainer Charles Milbank, winner of the Irish Oaks and the French Derby, who is a nephew of Sir Mark Milbank, 4th Baronet, formerly Master of the Queen's Household.

The present Baronet, Sir Anthony Milbank, succeeded his father, Sir Mark, in the title in 1984, though he gave up his career in the City some half-dozen years before in order to take on the running of Barningham. Since then he and his wife,

Belinda (a former event rider and daughter of the all-round sportsman Brigadier Adrian Gore), have carried out a major restoration of the house. Apart from tidying-up the north front, they have eradicated dry rot throughout and brought back authentic Georgian colour schemes.

The family holdings now comprise some 5,500 acres (of which 1,000 are farmed in hand) including about a quarter of the unspoilt Barningham village and extensive grouse moors. Sir Anthony is an enthusiastic Gun and enjoys fishing.

He manages the House Farm and estate himself, successfully combining agriculture and conservation and the Milbanks encourage as many different activities as possible to take place at Barningham. There are sheepdog trials, field trials, hunter trials, car and motorcycle rallies as well as cricket and football. The gardens, noted for the spectacular hillside rockery landscape early this century, are open several times for charity in summer.

Barningham Park, near Richmond, North Yorkshire, is not open to the public, though the gardens are open occasionally (as advertised).

Barningham: library.

FOLJAMBE OF OSBERTON

Osberton, Nottinghamshire: south front.

SET majestically in glorious parkland beside a lake, Osberton Hall near Worksop, in the northern tip of the old royal forest of Sherwood, could be described as an extension of the so-called 'Dukeries' to its south. Indeed the large agricultural and woodland estate shares a long boundary with Clumber Park, formerly seat of the Dukes of Newcastle. However, unlike many of the great ducal piles, Osberton is still in the private occupation of the Foljambes, the squire-archical family who commissioned William Wilkins, of National Gallery fame, to build the house in the early 1800s.

The present squire, Michael Foljambe, a popular figure in the world of eventing, is still, though in his fifties, an enthusiastic competitor in the sport, riding Galileo III and Luxide, despite a riding accident a few years ago. He was presented with the British Society Award of Merit for services to the British Horse Society, and the Osberton BHS Standard three-day event, usually held at the end of September, is very much a part of the equestrian calendar. The Princess Royal and Captain Mark Phillips have been frequent participants since the events began in 1969. The team selection trials for the 1976 Olympic Games at Montreal were held at Osberton.

The great park is in constant demand for various functions, which Mr Foljambe limits both in number and kind so as to avoid disturbing the heronry and other birds of many varieties which treat Osberton as a sanctuary for nesting and living. Nonetheless the place is used regularly for hunter trials, horse-driving trials, sheep-dog trials (with the profits going to the Guide Dogs for the Blind Association), Caravan Club weekends, Pony Club camps and the East Midland Dressage Group Horse Trials and members' training ground.

Mr Foljambe, who is a president of the Nottinghamshire branch of the Country Landowners Association and a past president of the Newark Show, won the Bledisloe Gold Medal in 1983 for his management of the 12,000-acre estate. Some 2,600 acres are farmed in hand under partnerships and the agricultural enterprise includes the distinguished Osberton herd of pedigree Jersey cattle which was established there as early as the 1880s.

Mr Foljambe, a qualified land agent and chartered surveyor, was educated at Eton and Magdalene College, Cambridge, where he read rural estate management and rode in occasional point-to-points. He did his National Service with the 15th/19th King's Royal Hussars in Germany. He inherited Osberton in 1960 on the death of his uncle, Captain Edmond Foljambe. The captain was a dedicated shooting man; his first wife, of Polish extraction, was a white huntress out in Kenya and his second wife, Judith Wright (a great-aunt of the Duchess of York), enjoys an outstanding reputation as a loader.

The Osberton estate has passed by inheritance for the last 300 years. At one time a property of the long-established Nottinghamshire family of Chaworth, it was acquired by the Bolles family in the 16th century. Thomas Bolles of Osberton recorded the family pedigree in the *Visitation of Nottinghamshire* in 1614. His second wife, Mary, was created a baronetess within nine months of his death in 1635. This is, in fact, the only case in

Opposite
Osberton: staircase and gallery.

Osberton: dining-room.

history of a baronetcy being conferred on a woman, although at the present time there is a baronetess by descent—Dame Maureen Daisy Helen Dunbar of Hempriggs.

The Bolles baronetcy passed to Dame Mary's son by her first marriage to Thomas Jobson (or Jopson), while Osberton went to her stepson, Samuel Bolles,

and thence to his daughter Mary Leek. In 1682 the Leeks exchanged Osberton for part of the Stow Park estate in Lincolnshire with the Thornhaghs from whome the Foljambes descend in the female line.

John Thornhagh-Hewett, MP for Nottinghamshire, was the principal witness at the trial of his neighbour the 'Wicked Lord' Byron (great-uncle of the poet) in the House of Lords in 1765 for killing his kinsman William Chaworth in a duel. Byron was found guilty of manslaughter but was discharged under the Statute of Privilege as a peer. During the 18th century Osberton was used only as a hunting box by the family or let out to tenants. However in the 1790s, following the death of his wife Arabella, the daughter and heiress of John Thornhagh-Hewett, Francis Ferrand Foljambe decided to make something more of Osberton.

The Foljambe family seat of Aldwarke near Rotherham was to become increasingly affected by industrialisation. They had come into Aldwarke through marriage to a Fitzwilliam heiress in the 16th century and had previously been seated at Walton Hall near Chesterfield, where Sir Godfrey Foljambe acted as one of the jailers of Mary Queen of Scots.

The Foljambes (pronounced '*Fulljum*') were originally an historic Derbyshire dynasty. Sir Thomas Foljambe was Bailiff for the High Peak in the 13th century and the family later held office under John of Gaunt and Henry VIII.

From about 1798 Francis Ferrand Foljambe, or 'FFF' as he is known at Osberton, set about improving the place. By enlarging an old pond that had been in front of nearby Scofton Hall he extended it to the north front of Osberton to create a spectacular lake. The new house, to Wilkins's design, incorporated part of an earlier dwelling of which only the cellar is still recognisable.

For that matter Wilkins's original designs (illustrated in G. Richardson's *New Vitruvius Britannicus*, 1808) largely disappeared under the later 19th-century alterations. He also designed a romantic folly to be built on the island in the lake for FFF's second wife, Lady Mary, daughter of the 4th Earl of Scarbrough.

The exceedingly handsome stables, which remain unchanged and much in use, are attributed to William Lindley, the Doncaster architect who died in 1818. FFF died four years earlier. He was succeeded by his grandson George Savile Foljambe, a noted collector of botanical and geological curiosities and a celebrated sportsman.

George's first wife, Harriet Milner, died shortly after giving birth to their son, Frank, in 1830 and in her memory he commissioned the architect Ambrose Poynter to build a private chapel (later a parish church for the estate). Sir Nikolaus Pevsner notes that it shows an early appreciation of the Norman style.

William Wilkins's original design for Osberton.

Poynter was called in again in the 1840s to build an extensive new service wing and an additional 'nursery floor' for George's children by his second wife, Lady Milton, a daughter of the 3rd (and last of that creation) Earl of Liverpool. The earldom was subsequently revived for their son Cecil, great-grandfather of the present Earl.

Osberton went to Cecil's elder half-brother, Frank, MP for East Retford, a Privy Councillor and Master of the Burton Hunt. He gave the interior of Osberton its pleasing and comfortable Victorian flavour, building out a large drawing-room and library with rooms over them to the north towards the lake and throwing together the old drawing-room and staircase hall to make an impressive central hall with a gallery. He abandoned Aldwarke, engulfed by sewage works and mines, which was pulled down in 1900.

The new north-west wing and the *porte-cochère* on the entrance front of Osberton were added to the designs of William Burn and his nephew McVicars Anderson. The present owner, Frank's great-grandson, has removed Poynter's top floor and half the length of the Wilkins service wing, so the house remains as completed by Anderson in the 1880s.

Besides sympathetically restoring the house Mr Foljambe has also tirelessly restored the park, church and estate which had suffered badly in the Second World War when Osberton was a military hospital. At present the future of the house is under discussion. Mr Foljambe, who is unmarried, has been considering various possibilities, including the use of the Hall as a sporting museum, a new British Equestrian Centre, as a centre for the Nature Conservation Movement or possibly part as a hospice. Whatever happens he is determined that the special character of the place will be preserved and that the Foljambes will remain at Osberton.

Group appointments and charity gatherings at Osberton, near Worksop, Nottinghamshire, are favourably considered and there are public functions such as the three-day events held on the estate (as advertised).

JAY OF DERNDALE

Thomas Jays XI, XII and XIII, plus Anne.

dated the one and twentieth day of October in the ninth year of the reign of King Charles (1634), Three Messauges and two yards land with the appurtenances called Eynons land lying in Brocton and Dernedall (*sic*) granted to the said Thomas and Katherine and Thomas and to the heirs of the said Katherine . . . the premises are clearly worth per annum £15.0s.0d.

THE Herefordshire Jays (*Homo sapiens*, not *Garrulus glandarius*) provide an object lesson in social history illustrating the survival of a dynasty of modest landowners for nearly four centuries. For the most part they have been not so much squires as 'squireens'—that useful Irish word coined to describe the least pretentious type of hereditary landed proprietor. Only in the early 19th century did the Jays aspire to something grander—and consequently nearly came a cropper—but happily their connection with Derndale, a family seat of unusual quaintness and intimacy, has remained unbroken.

Derndale, a small estate tucked away in one of the most beautiful parts of Herefordshire under Dinmore Hill, was formerly in the ownership of the Dean and Chapter of Hereford Cathedral. In the early 17th century the Jays seem to have acquired the copyhold of Derndale through marriage with the Wottons. Documents of 1577 and 1623 mention a 'John Wotton of Derndale'. The 'Katherine' mentioned in the *Parliamentary Survey* of 1649 (the Cromwellian 'Domesday') was presumably John Wotton's daughter. The Survey states that:

Thomas Jay and Katherine his wife and Thomas their son hold by copy of Court Roll

Thomas Jay is also among those listed as having to perform certain acts of husbandry for the owner of the manor of Canon Pyon and in return 'they are to have for their pains a piece of Beef and a Goose'.

At this stage the Jays would appear to have been yeomen farmers. In the 18th century they became more prosperous as tanners; the old bark barn still survives in the grounds at Derndale. The inventory compiled on the death of Thomas Jay IV in 1734 values his estate at £430. The items include hundreds of hides, barks and skins in the tanhouse and 'In the Syder House ffive hogsheds of Syder'.

The half-timbered 'Syder' or Cider House also remains as an evocative feature at Derndale. The estate is noted for its Kingston Black apples (the equivalent of Burgundy to cider-drinkers). A member of the family, William Jay of Lyde, was a key figure in the Herefordshire cider industry of the early 19th century and did much to improve the fruit. Today the Derndale apples go to Bulmers, the firm founded by a parson who lost a leg in a 19th-century Jay shooting party.

In the middle of the 18th century the Jay family fortunes received a further boost when a member of the Tomkin family, famous for its introduction of Herefords to this country, left the whole of his estate to 'Thomas Jay, tanner of Derndale'. This bequest and the marriage of Thomas Jay VI to Joanna Attwood from Tredington in Gloucestershire smoothed the advance of the Jays into the country gentry. In 1791, a year before his death, Thomas VI duly purchased the freehold of Derndale from the Dean and Chapter of Hereford Cathedral.

Thomas VI was probably responsible for putting the elegant 18th-century facade on to the 17th-century building. The wing containing the exceptionally handsome drawing-room was added in about 1810 by his upwardly mobile son and successor, Thomas Jay VII, who may also have laid out the grounds.

Thomas VII consolidated the Jays' position through his marriage to the well-to-do heiress Katherine Taylor from Tilling-

ton Court, whose father had been Mayor of Hereford and High Sheriff of the county. Thomas himself served as High Sheriff in 1812; his procession of carriages and horses to meet the judge coming from Shrewsbury Assizes was the longest on record, stretching for more than two miles.

An active magistrate, Thomas Jay VII became a prominent figure in Herefordshire. In politics he was an ardent Whig whose influence would sway a county election. Abandoning the family tanning operations at Derndale, he decided to finance the Hereford City and County Bank in partnership with Squire Bodenham of Rotherwas.

In the best traditions of the squirearchy, Thomas VII evinced a practical concern for the poor and needy and for the education of their children. He was also an enthusiastic sportsman, maintaining a pack of harriers at Derndale where some of the kennels still stand. Nothing daunted, his wife kept a pet hare which used to lie on the dining-room hearth at night.

Jay's Bank, like so many other similar enterprises at that time, was badly affected by the deflation of the post-Napoleonic Wars period. Finally, in 1828, the business collapsed. Poor Jay and Bodenham found themselves having to pay the creditors 20 shillings in the pound. This disaster broke more than the Bank. Thomas VII died a year later, aged 53, leaving the family in the financial soup.

Much of the estate had to be sold, the eldest son (Thomas VIII) died shortly afterwards, the second son emigrated to Australia and Derndale was let out, its contents dispersed. Before his death, Thomas VIII, a solicitor, had forecast 'great difficulty' in letting Derndale: 'The House is so much too large for a farmer, and not sufficiently modern for a gentleman of the present day and will cost much money to furnish it.' Nonetheless, Derndale was let to the Clark (formerly Onions) family by Thomas VIII's widow, an Evans, and later by her spinster daughter, Mary.

The Jay features are clearly delineated in the bust of Mary's uncle and sometime man of affairs James Jay, a solicitor and noted shot, in the staircase hall at Derndale. Thomas Jay XII, son of the present head of the family, bears a striking resemblance to this bust. Among James Jay's descendants, incidentally, is the actress Rachel Kempson, widow of Sir Michael Redgrave.

Upon her death in 1907 Miss Jay bequeathed Derndale to her cousin Thomas Jay X, a grandson of the cider improver, William Jay of Lyde. Thomas X, then 36, had married Gertrude Reese (whose father owned Urishay Castle and Cabalva in Wales) and established a family business in Chichester.

As his son Thomas Jay XI points out, a lesser man than his father would have sold the property without hesitation. However, on his first visit to Derndale to view his inheritance, he was entranced by the view of the flowerbeds on the lawn as he came down the drive. 'This Victorian feature, together with the general charm of the place and family pride, made him determined to live there,' Thomas XI recalls.

And so, after 80 years, the Jays returned to Derndale. Until his death in 1948, Thomas Jay X dedicated himself wholeheartedly to the restoration of the house, the retrieval of many objects previously associated with it and the resurgence of the estate. A keen shooting man, Thomas X, according to his son, 'practically never left the house without a gun'. He was a stalwart attender of the local Woolhope Club meetings and a fund of local history and folklore.

Thomas Jay XI has continued the family's yacht business, Jay Marine of Chichester, and sat as a JP for West Sussex. He brought the gates at Derndale from Chichester. Educated at Bromsgrove, the Worcestershire public school, he served in the Second World War with the Royal Sussex Regiment. His wife, Alexandra, is the daughter of the late Walter Shippam, founding father of the well-known potted meat empire.

Thomas Jay XII followed his father to Bromsgrove and worked for Shippams and raced Minis before taking over the running of the family farm in 1974. In addition to the cider apples the enterprise also includes grassland and corn. Thomas XII and his younger brother, James, continue the shooting spirit of the Jays.

With the exception of Miss Mary Jay, when the entail was broken, Derndale has been in the possession of a Thomas Jay since the 1630s. Miss Jay's heir, from the junior line, happened to be called Thomas after his own maternal grandfather Thomas Death, an Alderman of the city of London. The tradition is all set to continue: the young son of Thomas XII and his wife, Janet (née Warner, from Tewkesbury), is the 13th Thomas Jay of Derndale.

Opposite
Derndale, drawing-room.

Derndale, near Canon Pyon, Herefordshire, is not open to the public, though local events are occasionally held in the grounds (as advertised).

STEUART FOTHRINGHAM OF MURTHLY

Murthly Castle, Perthshire: east front

AN increasingly important role for country houses is as the setting for concerts or other manifestations of the arts. Frequently these shows are part of a local festival which is considerably enhanced by featuring the nearest 'big house' on its programme. By no means every family seat is blessed with a large enough room for such events but the charming early-Victorian music room at Murthly Castle in Perthshire is ideal for the purpose.

Murthly's owner, Robert Scrymsoure Steuart Fothringham of Pourie and Murthly, is himself a keen musician and a particular devotee of chamber music. It was in the music room at Murthly that Freddy Stockdale's enterprising Lincolnshire-based Pavilion Opera touring company gave its first performance in Scotland a few years ago. Murthly is also the setting for concerts forming part of the Dunkeld and Birnam Arts Festival.

Formerly a chartered accountant in the City of London, Mr Steuart Fothringham and his wife, Elizabeth (*née* Lawther) returned to Scotland in the late 1960s. Shortly afterwards he took over the running of the Fothringham estate from his father, the late Major Thomas Steuart Fothringham, and of the Murthly estate from his bachelor uncle, the late Donald Steuart Fothringham, a much-loved laird who made light of his blindness.

The Pourie and Fothringham estates in Angus have been owned by the Fothringhams since at least the 15th century, whereas Robert's grandfather, Lieutenant-Colonel Walter Steuart Fothringham, who was Vice-Lieutenant of Perthshire, inherited the Murthly property in 1890 upon the death of his kinsman Sir Douglas Stewart, 8th and last Baronet.

Today the Murthly estate extends to 14,000 acres, of which about 4,000 are woodland, 1,700 low ground farmed in hand (beef and barley) and 2,800 acres hill (sheep). Gloriously situated on the south side of the River Tay, Murthly is celebrated for its trees which include some giant Douglas firs. About half the 4,000 acres of woodland are dedicated to commercial forestry. At the castle there is a remarkable 'wood museum' which Walter Steuart Fothringham formed using examples of the different types of timber from the estate in the early years of this century.

The 'policies', as the Scots say, were principally laid out in the 1840s by the colourful Sir William Drummond Stewart, 7th Baronet, newly returned from his adventures in America. He brought back three Red Indian servants, the artist Alfred Jacob Miller (who painted evocative scenes of the Wild West), a small herd of buffalo and a cornucopia of trees, shrubs and plants. The Red Indians did not, apparently, stay the course but the buffalo were enclosed in a large park a couple of miles from the castle surrounded by a high stone wall. Unfortunately, the wall does not seem to have been strong enough as the beasts frequently escaped. On one occasion they are said to have held up the Royal Mail for 48 hours.

Sir William landscaped the trees and shrubs in splendid terraces and avenues which can still be seen though they are now well past their best.

The Murthly gardens are opened occasionally to the public under Scotland's Gardens Scheme, of whose executive Mr Steuart Fothringham is a member. He was also secretary of the Historic Houses Association for Scotland from 1976 until 1983, during which time the membership of this admirable 'trades union' of private owners virtually doubled. He is a Deputy Lieutenant for Angus and a member of the Queen's Bodyguard for Scotland (Royal Company of Archers).

The Archers, for all their stylish uniforms, are much more than ceremonial adjuncts of the Scottish Court; the noble art of archery is still faithfully practised by the Company's members and Mr Steuart Fothringham is a distinguished exponent, having twice won the Queen's Prize for archery at the Palace of Holyroodhouse in the 1970s.

Beside his skill with a bow and an arrow (doubtless something of which his Wild West predecessor would have approved), the present laird of Murthly is also a keen shot and fisherman. At present all the six low-ground beats (pheasant and only a few grouse) are let out to an American company but the fishing (three miles of the Tay) is in hand and is let by the day.

Mrs Steuart Fothringham looks after the holiday cottage enterprise on the estate and takes a special interest in the

interior decoration of the castle which is currently undergoing extensive renovation following an outbreak of dry rot. She and her husband have four children: Thomas and Lionel (a budding musician), both at Eton, and Mariana and Ilona.

When Mariana was at North Foreland Lodge School, she compiled a record of

Above
Murthly: garden house and arched yews.

Below
Murthly: south (garden) front.

Murthly: interior of mid 19th-century chapel.

the castle's buildings for her History of Art A level—an extremely worthwhile exercise which has become something of a habit among the younger generation at family seats.

Murthly's architectural history certainly needs some unravelling as there have been numerous additions and alterations over five centuries. The castle seems to have begun life in about 1450 as a simple keep with a parapeted flat roof and a spiral staircase. About a century later another tower was added with crow-stepped gables and angle turrets. In the 1660s a three-storey wing was extended to the east

from the 16th-century tower and another wing was added to the north. It was also in the 1660s that the formal gardens near the castle, containing a charming garden house, were first laid out.

Early in the 18th century the north wing was extended and in about 1790 the castle acquired its elegantly Adamesque entrance, with a pediment and double-sweep staircase up to the front door. Early in the 19th century the north (service) wing was further extended and then, following a fire in 1848, the east wing was largely rebuilt and extended still further.

The story goes that Sir William Steuart

(or Stewart), 11th laird of Grantully (an estate some 15 miles to the west now owned by Robert's brother, Henry Steuart Fothringham), acquired Murthly by distinctly dubious means in the early 17th century. A Gentleman of the Bedchamber (and, some say, 'whipping boy') to James VI, Sir William is supposed to have accused his kinsman Abercrombie of Murthly of sheltering Jesuits at the castle but promised to keep quiet about it if Abercrombie would agree to sell him Murthly for an absurdly low figure.

The castle was enlarged and embellished in the 1660s by Sir William's son, Sir Thomas Stewart ('a knight of somewhat grim aspect but gorgeous in his apparel'). The Fothringhams descend from Sir Thomas's second daughter, Marjory Stewart, who married David Fothringham of Pourie, a champion gentleman rider.

In 1720 Murthly passed to a cousin, Sir George Stewart, 2nd Baronet (whose father, an eminant lawyer, had been created a baronet in 1683). His descendant Sir John Drummond Stewart, 6th Baronet, who succeeded to Murthly in 1827, was a connoisseur and art collector. Fresh from his Grand Tour he determined to build an amazing new castle, the completion of which would be followed by the demolition of the old one.

As things turned out, it was the old castle that remained standing and the new one was razed to the ground. Happily, however, a fascinating picture at Murthly records the spectacular juxtaposition of the two structures (see FRONTISPIECE).

Sir John commissioned the Gothic Revival architect James Gillespie Graham to build 'the largest private house in Scotland' but, although the building was finished outside by the time of the 6th Baronet's early death in 1838, the interior was never completed. The 'New Castle' stood empty and forlorn—its basement used as an estate workshop and garage—until Donald Steuart Fothringham put it out of its magnificent misery in 1949.

Sir John was succeeded in the baronetcy by his brother William, a veteran of Waterloo who had amassed a fortune in furs, railroads and other wheezes out in America. The problem was that William, who detested his elder brother, had vowed never to sleep again under the roof of Murthly. This little local difficulty was overcome by the extension of the east wing to include a new bedroom and the castle's only bathroom, boasting a handsome marble tub still *in situ*. The

servants are supposed to have been given instructions to rouse Sir William should he nod off in any other part of the old castle.

The appearance of the elaborate ballroom, complete with blue and gold 'bee' ceiling, and the music room, with its ceiling painted by Soderini, dates from Sir William's time—though it is probable that these lavish interiors were originally intended for the new castle.

A. W. Pugin had a hand in their design and also in the even more impressive interior of the chapel in the grounds which boasts a stained glass rose window and a mural depicting the *Vision of Constantine* by William Christie. Both the Christie and Soderini's *Bacchus and Ariadne* in the music room have recently been restored

Murthly Castle, Murthly, Perthshire, is open by appointment to groups.

by Anthea Pelham Burn.

The chapel, also designed by Gillespie Graham, was the first Roman Catholic place of worship to be dedicated in Scotland since the Reformation. Sir William had been received into the Catholic church in New Orleans; the Fothringham's Catholicism stems from the present laird's mother who was a Noel of the Gainsborough family.

For all its extraordinary diversity and exoticism, Murthly does not, as Mariana Steuart Fothringham observes, 'appear odd in any way but on the contrary surprisingly harmonious in style'.

Robert Steuart Fothringham of Pourie and Murthly.

GORDON-DUFF OF DRUMMUIR

Mr and Mrs Alex Gordon-Duff with their children.

ANYONE with a sense of tradition holds a special affection for the smaller counties of the British Isles. Posterity will surely never forgive Messrs Heath and Walker for destroying the old counties of England and Wales in the 1970s and introducing absurd new boundaries that are, in the words of the late Peter Fleetwood-Hesketh, 'non-historical, unnatural, illogical, far from practical, as well as being offensive to the people'. Although Scotland is now divided up into lumpish 'regions', at least the old county names—such as the smallest of them all, Clackmannanshire—have been retained within these administrative structures.

Among the most attractive of small Scottish counties is Banffshire, a division of the Grampian Region, which stretches for a mere 50 or so miles between Aberdeenshire and the counties of Moray and Inverness in the north-east maritime corner of the country. Colonel T. R. ('Robin') Gordon-Duff, late of the Rifle Brigade and the Gordon Highlanders (TA), recently served 22 years as Lord-Lieutenant of Banffshire. Both his grand-father and great-grandfather were Vice-Lieutenants of Banffshire, while his great-great-grandfather, like himself, served as convener (or chairman) of the county.

Indeed one of the family's disgruntled neighbours once described Banffshire as a 'Duff-ridden county'. A village near Drummuir Castle, the family seat, is called Dufftown.

The Duffs acquired the Drummuir estate in 1621 from Robert Innes of Invermarkie and Balvenie (later created a Baronet), the son of one of the murderers of the 'Bonnie' Earl of Moray. The purchaser was Adam Duff, 4th laird of Torriesul, who had married Jean Gordon of Abergeldie.

The Duffs of Drummuir's son and heir, 'Robert the Gallant', as he is known in the family, was killed at the Battle of Alford in July 1645, fighting for Lord Montrose's Cavalier army which routed the Covenanters outside Aberdeen.

Robert the Gallant's son, Adam Duff, who built the Mains of Drummuir in about 1670, died in 1682, leaving a daughter by his wife, Anne Abercromby. The story goes that he advised his daughter, Catherine, that she could marry anyone she liked so long as he had plenty of cash and was called Duff.

Catherine dutifully obliged by marrying Alexander Duff (no apparent close relation), the son of the Provost of Inverness. Described by a contemporary as 'a conscientious, good-natured and honest man', Alexander was MP for Inverness from 1702 until the Act of Union and then sat in the first Union Parliament.

The next laird, known at Drummuir as 'Mad Robert', appears to have confined his activities to playing chess and cards. By the time of his son, Archibald, who succeeded to the estate in 1735, the Mains of Drummuir was in considerable disrepair and he built Kirkton House, close to the site of the present castle, which he referred to as his 'little log cabin in the woods'.

Archibald Duff, a barrister of the Inner Temple and a bachelor, died in 1788 and was succeeded at Drummuir by his cousin

John, another bachelor. Although a Captain in the 93rd Regiment, from which he retired in 1798, John does not seem to have been made of such stern stuff. According to the family chronicles he was 'frightened away by a fall of snow' and fled to the Continent. He lived mainly in Switzerland and France and died in Paris in 1836.

Meanwhile, the Drummuir estate had been taken in hand by his brother, the redoubtable Vice-Admiral Archibald Duff, whose naval uniform with the short-lived red-facings of William IV's time is preserved in the castle. The Admiral was an independent-minded character of radical views and much ingeniosity. He invented a new form of gun-sight for ships and built a harbour to his own revolutionary design, with a concave surface.

He was also a noted agricultural improver and received a silver plate from the Highland Society for draining a large piece of marshland at Drummuir in 1828.

Twenty years later, as if to round off his achievements, he decided to build a Gothic baronial castle, complete with banner and corner towers, turrets and a *porte-cochère*, at Drummuir. In his 75th year the childless Admiral chose a virgin site with splendid views across the Strathisla valley and commissioned the Elgin architect Thomas Mackenzie to erect a suitably impressive granite pile.

Most of the interior is as the Admiral left it at his death in 1858. The light and elegant drawing-rooms, the panelled dining-room, with its family portraits, and the imposing staircase hall show the early Scottish Victorian style at its best.

The service wing, to the right of the entrance front, was added shortly after the Admiral's death by his cousin and successor Lachlan Gordon-Duff. The surname of Gordon had descended with the feudal barony of Park through the Admiral's stepmother, Helen Gordon.

Lachlan, a Major in the 20th Regiment and MP for Banffshire from 1857 to 1861, decided it was more practicable to flood the marshland which his cousin the Admiral had previously drained, to create the loch now known as Loch Park. He continued the Duff traditions of public service and conscientious landownership, though his life was blighted by the death of his adored daughter, Mary, aged 16, in 1868.

Forty years on we find Mary's brother, Thomas, complaining about Drummuir being an impossible house, built by 'two old men', full of dry rot and fit only to be pulled down. Nonetheless, in true Edwardian manner, he converted the old library into a billiard room. The present library was formerly the breakfast room.

Drummuir Castle, Banffshire: garden front.

Right
Drummuir: entrance front.

Above
View of Strathisla Valley from roof of Drummuir.

Drummuir Castle, near Keith, Banffshire, is not open to the public at present but can be visited in the summer months through Grampian Rail Tours (as advertised).

Both Thomas and his sister, Helen, married children of the rich Glasgow chemical manufacturer Sir Charles Tennant Bt, of Glen, founder of the fashionable artistic and intellectual dynasty prominent in the coterie known as the 'Souls'. Thomas's wife, Posy, eldest sister of the incorrigible Margot Asquith, was a consumptive and consequently she and Thomas lived mainly abroad, in South Africa, until her death in 1888.

Thomas later married Mildred Walker, a steel heiress. They were appointed CBE and OBE respectively for their work for the Red Cross in the First World War. Thomas's only son by his marriage to Posy Tennant, Lachlan, had been killed with the Gordon Highlanders in 1914.

Between the wars Drummuir was let out as a shooting lodge and during hostilities it was requisitioned by the military. However, in 1946 Lachlan's son Robin and his wife, Jean (*née* Moir), returned to the castle, taking up residence on the first floor.

Mrs Gordon-Duff died in 1981 and in 1985 the Colonel moved out of the castle to settle at Kirkton House in the grounds. Since then their son, Alex, and his wife, Priscilla (*née* Brereton), have been tackling the formidable job of restoration and renovation. The first stage is to rewire, eliminate dry rot and to create a new kitchen ('Every generation puts in a new kitchen,' Mrs Gordon-Duff says) and estate office in the service wing. Next the roof needs attention and then the first floor will be reconverted.

The commendably enthusiastic young Gordon-Duffs met at Durham University and married in 1973. They have four children: Laura, Torquil and the twins, Adam and Jemima. Alex Gordon-Duff is a chartered surveyor, who trained with Smiths Gore at Fochabers and is a member of the Prince's Trust for the Grampian Region. The estate now extends to about 10,000 acres, of which 1,600 are devoted to forestry and 800 are farmed in hand (sheep, cows and arable).

Among the crops produced are organic oats for a new enterprise on the estate, the Mill of Towie, an 19th-century building with a working mill-wheel. The Grainstore Restaurant, under Mrs Gordon-Duff's management, serves local produce (not forgetting this is 'whisky country') which is excellently cooked and warmly recommended.

Other projects to help keep Drummuir going include a possible Clan MacDuff museum in the capacious basement and the use of the castle for entertaining and for fishing and shooting parties. The shooting (a few grouse and plenty of pheasant) is in hand and some 25 days are let each season. As far as tourism is concerned, Drummuir has the good fortune to be on the delightful branch line which runs from Aberdeen to Dufftown. A visit to the castle is an occasional feature of the Grampian Rail Tours' excursions to the Glenfiddich Distillery.

PART III

THE 18th AND 19th CENTURIES

PLUMPTRE
OF GOODNESTONE

Goodnestone Park, Kent: Oval Room.

'WE WERE at a ball on Saturday ...,' wrote Jane Austen to her sister, Cassandra, in 1796. 'We dined at Goodnestone and in the evening danced two country dances ... I opened the ball with Edward Bridges.' This is merely one of many references to Goodnestone Park, Kent, and her Bridges connections in the letters of the great novelist. Jane often stayed with her brother, Edward Austen (later Knight), and his wife, Elizabeth (*née* Bridges), at a pleasant house on the Goodnestone estate, called Rowling, before they moved to Godmersham Park in 1812. The 'Edward Bridges' Jane mentions was the eldest son of Sir Brook Bridges, 3rd Baronet, the squire of Goodnestone, by his wife, Fanny, (*née* Fowler), co-heiress to the ancient Barony of FitzWalter and descendant of the foremost baronial enforcer of *Magna Carta*.

The Goodnestone (pronounced '*Gunston*') estate was bought from the Engeham family in 1700 by the 3rd Baronet's great-grandfather, Brook Bridges.

Opposite
Goodnestone: south front.

96

Goodnestone: view to church through walled garden.

pediment on the principal (east) front; the exterior was apparently rendered in stucco.

The ground-floor rooms on the east front almost certainly show the hand of Robert Mylne, one of a remarkable Scots dynasty of architects and master-masons who also worked at Loton, Shropshire (*see* PART I). Celebrated for his remodelling of Inveraray Castle, Mylne made designs for 'many improvements' at Goodnestone in 1770. His work is likely to have included the prettily painted Oval Room and the rooms flanking this with curved walls at either end and classically decorated doorcases.

The second, (and last), remodelling was carried out from 1844 to 1845 by Sir Brook William Bridges, 5th Baronet (the nephew of Jane Austen's dancing partner) to the designs of Rickman and Hussey of Birmingham. This involved switching the entrance front from the east to the west. The west front acquired a giant Doric portico, while a swaggering cartouche of arms was inserted in the pediment on the east. At the same time, the original brick was uncovered and the main facades were adorned with stone windowcases.

A few years earlier, the 5th Baronet, a Tory politician and friend of Disraeli's, had attampted to claim the abeyant Fitz-Walter Barony. Unfortunately, as *The Complete Peerage* observes, Sir Brook's politics ensured the rejection of this claim. 'The Whig Ministry of the early Victorian period,' it notes sarcastically, 'were scrupulously careful not to allow any considerations of equity or desert . . .'

By way of compensation, some quarter of a century later, Sir Brook was given a new creation of a FitzWalter Barony by letters patent, only for this title to expire with him upon his death without children in 1875. Moreover, the baronetcy did not survive much longer, dying out with his childless brother in 1890.

The Goodnestone estate was then inherited by the sister of the last two baronets, Eleanor, the wife of the Reverend Henry Plumptre. The Plumptres' grandson, another Henry (a bearded, balding figure sometimes mistaken for Edward VII) decided to try to revive the historic Barony of FitzWalter.

In 1924 he was successful, and was summoned to Parliament by writ as the 20th Baron, thereby ending 168 years of abeyance. But, despite marrying twice (he was, in fact, the first man to take advantage of the Act enabling one to marry one's deceased wife's sister), he also died child-

Originally from Worcestershire, Bridges held the post of Auditor of the Imprest in the Treasury for 33 years, having been first appointed by Charles II in 1672. The present house dates from the early 1700s (a brick on the east front has '1704' scratched upon it) and was built according to the familiar 'double-pile' formula pioneered by Sir Roger Pratt at Coleshill in the 1650s. As erected, it had two storeys above a basement, and an attic with dormer windows. The splendid oak staircase is contemporary with the original building.

According to Hasted's *History and Survey of Kent*, which illustrates a late-18th-century engraving of Devis's watercolour of the house, Sir Brook Bridges, 3rd Baronet and a cultivated classicist, 're-built' Goodnestone. The remodelling was drastic. The house was considerably enlarged and acquired a third storey and a

less, in 1932, and so the title became dormant.

The next chapter in this baronial chronicle came 21 years later when the 20th Lord FitzWalter's nephew, Brook Plumptre, successfully revived the title to become the 21st Baron. Brought up in South Africa (where his parents had emigrated), the present Lord FitzWalter served in the Second World War as a captain in the Buffs. His wife, Margaret, is a member of the well-known Kent family of Deedes (and sister of the former Cabinet Minister and Editor of *The Daily Telegraph*, Lord Deedes); also a descendent of Sir Brook Bridges, 3rd Baronet, and Fanny Fowler, through the female line.

Meanwhile, the future of Goodnestone was uncertain. It had been requisitioned by the Army during the Second World War and remained in military occupation until 1949. In 1955 Lord and Lady FitzWalter, then living in a farmhouse on the estate, decided to move back into the big house.

Four years later, while the FitzWalter's son, George, aged three, was enjoying his midday nap, disaster struck. Goodnestone was nearly consumed in a conflagration that destroyed the roof and gutted much of the upper two floors. Fortunately, however, the ground-floor rooms and the family portraits—not to mention young George—survived unscathed.

Since the fire, the FitzWalters have undertaken a major restoration, including the complete rebuilding of the roof. Much work has also been done outside (with the help of the redoubtable head gardener, John Wellard) to make Goodnestone one of the most lovely gardens in Kent. Unfortunately, the 17th-century Well House, which used to stand to the northwest of the house, had to be demolished in 1965 as it had become structurally unsafe; but the enchanting four-acre walled garden leading down to the village church is the epitome of the old-fashioned English garden. Of particular architectural interest in the walled garden, laid out in the 18th century, are the two rusticated arches faced with flint. For garden enthusiasts, Lady FitzWalter's old-fashioned roses are well worth journeying to see.

Those who think of Kent as a suburban county will also be pleasantly surprised by the benevolently squirearchical set up at Goodnestone, with its picturesque estate village, complete with the FitzWalter Arms and a newly laid out cricket ground. Today the estate consists of 2,500 acres, 1,500 of which are farmed in hand (mixed

arable). There are pedigree Sussex cattle bought by Lady FitzWalter and known as the Deedestone Herd. A small syndicate shoots over the estate and the West Street Foxhounds meet here at the end of the shooting season. Eleven people are employed on the farms, six on the estate and gardens.

Naturally enough, the Goodnestone gardens, which open to the public on a regular basis, feature in *Collins' Book of British Gardens* by the third of the FitzWalters' five sons, George Plumptre. He defines Goodnestone's charm as 'a nostalgic quality arising from the harmony between the old house and its surrounding trees and lawns . . .'. He and his wife, Alexandra, make their home at Rowling, the house where another author associated with the family used to stay a couple of centuries ago.

Lord FitzWalter outside entrance front of Goodnestone.

Goodnestone Park, near Canterbury, Kent: the house is not open to the public, though the gardens are open regularly as advertised.

BURRELL OF KNEPP CASTLE

Sir Walter and Lady Burrell.

Opposite
Knepp Castle, Sussex: entrance front.

Amerom the estate papers at Knepp Castle near West Grinstead in the Sussex Weald, the seat of the Burrell baronets, is a note that Sir Charles Burrell 'consulted Mr Nash, an Architect of eminence who furnished him with a plan for the building'. With its grandiose turrets and round tower, in a picturesque setting by a large lake, Knepp is one of the most pleasing, and least known, compositions by John Nash, best known as the Prince Regent's architect.

The first of the Burrell family recorded as living in Sussex was the Reverend Gerard Burrell (youngest son of Sir John Burrell, a Devonian and veteran of the Battle of Agincourt), who became Archdeacon of Chichester and Vicar of Cuckfield, where he died in 1509. The original family seat, Ockenden Manor in Cuckfield, still belongs the the Burrells and is now a hotel. In the middle of the 18th century Merrik Burrell became Governor of the Bank of England, was made a baronet and bought the West Grinstead Park estate.

Sir Merrick was a bachelor and left the property to his great-nephew, Walter

Knepp: staircase and chandelier.

Beside the Worthing road which runs along the Knepp estate is a fragment of a Norman keep—the remains of an old castle probably built in the 11th century by the de Braose family. Sir Charles Burrell's new Knepp Castle was built between 1809 and 1812 at a cost of £28,500, of which £9,500 was for decorations. The building work was executed to Nash's design by Alexander Kyffin. Most of the exterior was rendered in stucco, incised to imitate stone blocks.

Whereas Knepp's exterior has a flamboyantly rambling quality, the interior is strictly disciplined, providing a most pleasing sequence of rooms. The hexagonal vestibule leads to an octagonal hall, beyond which is a circular stairwell. The superb, cantilevered staircase, with a cast-iron handrail, has a large three-dimensional Gothic window half-way up. Knepp's secret is that it is a medium-sized country house disguised as a castle.

Sir Charles Burrell, who was MP for Shoreham for 55 years and 'Father of the House', inherited West Grinstead Park from his bachelor brother Walter in 1831, combining the two properties in an estate of some 5,000 acres. The house was sold to the racehorse owner J. P. Hornung in 1912. Eighty years earlier Knepp Castle had suffered a fire which gutted the front of the building and destroyed many family treasures, including eight pictures by Holbein.

The present baronet, Sir Walter Burrell, was a month old when the fire occurred. Many owners would have abandoned the castle after such a disaster but Sir Walter's father, Sir Merrik Burrell, set out to recreate the Gothic decoration as accurately as possible. He succeeded triumphantly. The pretty friezes were reinstated and sympathetic new features included a number of good late-18th-century chimneypieces from Irish Georgian country houses that had suffered in the Troubles; the mid-17th-century panelling and chimneypiece in the parlour; and the fine mid-19th-century chandelier in the staircase hall which came from Dorchester House in London.

The redecoration was continued by the present baronet, who married Judith Denman, a grand-daughter of the 1st Viscount Cowdrey in 1931. Lady Cowdray renovated some of the upstairs rooms as a wedding present. Lady Burrell's contribution includes a delightful 1930s 'modern' bathroom with an ironwork balcony painted red. Further restoration and redecoration were necessary after the Sec-

Burrell, who pulled down the old house and built a new one to the designs of John Nash. West Grinstead Park—which eventually became part of the National Stud and was pulled down in 1970, riddled with dry rot—so impressed Walter's brother, Sir Charles Burrell, owner of the neighbouring Knepp estate, that he commissioned Nash to design something grander for himself.

Charles and Walter were the two elder sons of Sir William Burrell of Deepdene near Dorking, the celebrated antiquary who collected a mass of important material (now in the British Musuem) for a history of Sussex. Under a special remainder Sir William inherited a baronetcy, and the Knepp estate from his father-in-law, Sir Charles Raymond. Sir William's youngest son, Percy, commemorated by a portrait in the castle, was killed in 1807 when British forces were defeated by General Belgrano in Buenos Aires.

ond World War when the castle had been requisitioned by the Army.

To help pay for the upkeep some outlying parts of the castle have been converted into a maisonette and two flats. The estate is a settlement under trustees and now consists of about 4,000 acres, including about 400 acres of dedicated woodland. The Home Farm is about 800 acres, of which half is under winter wheat and barley and leys.

The Burrells are a distinguished agricultural dynasty. The story goes that the castle's builder, Sir Charles, was jealous not only of his brother's house but also of his herd of fallow deer, and so bought a flock of four-horned black and white Jacob sheep. 'They are less expensive to fence in,' comments Sir Walter who, like his father Sir Merrik, is a past president of the Royal Agricultural Society of England.

Sir Merrik started a herd of dual-purpose red poll cattle which now consists of two dairy herds of some 100 each. The estate has also recently started a bull-beef unit. The Knepp herd has been prominent in the show ring and young bulls have been widely exported.

The Knepp woodland won the 1983 Royal Agricultural Society of England competition for the best-managed woodland of fewer than 450 acres and also a prize for the best hardwood plantation. 'The woodlands are commercially run, but combined with amenity, shooting and hunting and the preservation and extension of bird and animal habitats,' Sir Walter says. The land is too flat to show high sporting birds but rabbits remain in sufficient numbers to provide excellent shooting.

The 50-acre lake, originally an Elizabethan hammer-pond, is used for duck shooting and is a favourite haunt for birdwatchers. 'The policy is to rear as many ducks as we shoot and these help to attract the wild ones as well as teal, widgeon, pochard, tufted and other fowl in the winter,' Sir Walter says. Herons have nested in old oak trees beside the lake for the past ten years.

The Burrells own the Crawley and Horsham Hunt Kennels and the opening meet is held at the castle. Sir Walter's younger son, Mark, who owns the Dragons Estate nearby, is the third generation of the family to act as Field-Master. One of the estate tenants has recently started a pack of mink hounds.

Sir Walter Burrell is the senior Deputy-Lieutenant for West Sussex and was vice-chairman of the county council for many years. His local appointments have included the chairmanship of the North West Sussex Water Board. At a national level, Sir Walter played a leading part, together with the late Sir Richard Proby, in the resurgence of the Country Landowners Association after the Second World War. He was closely involved in the landlord and tenant legislation incorporated in the 1948 Agriculture Acts and was president of the CLA in 1952. In the 1960s he became chairman of the RASE and helped establish the permanent site at Stoneleigh, now the National Agriculture Centre.

Sir Walter and Lady Burrell now have 14 grandchildren and six great-grandchildren. Their elder son lives in Australia where he farms some 6,000 acres, but the rest of the family are based in Sussex. The impressive Nash Castle, glorious landscape and model estate make Knepp a consummate English family seat.

Knepp: chimneypiece in dining-room.

Knepp Castle, near West Grinstead, West Sussex, is not open to the public though applications by specialised groups for appointments are considered by the estate office.

COOKSON OF MELDON

Mr and Mrs Michael Cookson.

O N 'the most beautiful November day' he had ever known, Colonel John Cookson, of Meldon in Northumberland, celebrated his 80th birthday in a style befitting a foxhunting squire 'blooded' in 1909. The Morpeth (the local hunt founded by the Cooksons, who have provided most of its Masters) met that day at Meldon Park. A large Field attended and the Colonel, on his cob, Nutty, rode through the front door of the Greek Revival family seat into the majestic Staircase Hall.

'I saw that the front door was open,' Colonel Cookson recalls. 'Nutty put his head through and then I thought—why not?' His son, the present squire of Meldon and Joint-Master of the Morpeth, Michael Cookson, affectionately submits that it was not so much done on impulse as the preconceived fulfilment of a long-held ambition.

According to Hodgson's *History of Northumberland*, the now vanished old house, Meldon Tower, originally a seat of the Herons of Ford Castle, was in the village about a mile away from today's Meldon Park. In the mid-17th century the Meldon estate became part of the large Derwentwater landholdings when the

Fenwick heiress married Francis Rad-clyffe, 1st Earl of Derwentwater.

The Earldon was attained and the estates forfeited in 1716 when the 3rd Earl was executed for having taken part in the preceding year's Jacobite Rebellion. The Meldon section of the estate was among the property subsequently settled as an endowment on the Royal Hospital for Seamen at Greenwich.

In 1832 the Greenwich Hospital Trust sold the Meldon estate ('consisting of 2,070 acres, including 171 acres of plantation and woods . . .' yielding a rental of £2,119 per annum) to Isaac Cookson, a younger son of a prominent Newcastle banker. Originally from Cumberland, the Cooksons had settled in Newcastle in the late 17th century when the family fortunes were established by the first Isaac Cookson, a merchant adventurer. Their seat in County Durham, Whitehill, was bought in 1745.

The family have long been to the fore on the Turf. There is a picture at Meldon of Joseph Cookson's Diamond being narrowly beaten by Harry Tempest-Vane's Hambletonian in a famous match run at Newmarket for 3,000 guineas in 1799; the previous season however, Mr Cookson had won the Derby with Sir Harry. In more recent times Colonel John Cookson's home-bred horse Meldon broke the mile record on the old course at Ascot in winning the Rous Memorial Stakes in 1957.

The pre-eminent Newcastle architect at the time of Isasc Cookson's purchase of the Meldon estate in 1832 was John Dobson, a prolific and remarkably economic performer much in demand among the north-eastern gentry. As well as designing several new houses he also remodelled more than 30 seats in the area. Clearly he was the man for the job of building Meldon Park. In the authoritative view of Mark Girouard, the result remains 'perhaps the best example of Dobson's competence as an architect of country houses'.

Upon receiving the commission, Dobson examined the estate for a month before choosing a picturesque site on a ledge above a valley sweeping down to the Wansbeck in the north half of the old enclosed 466-acre deer park. He designed the south front, with a central bay window, to face the view across the valley and the entrance front, with an Ionic porch, to the west.

A service wing (shortened in 1962) stretches out to the north; while on the east side is the recently restored conserva-

Opposite
Meldon Park, Northumberland.

tory and soon-to-be restored billiards room in a wing looking south over a small formal garden by the east facade of the house. A watercolour perspective painted by Dobson is preserved at Meldon; as are his estimates of June 1832 amounting to £7,188.1s.11d. (which did not include the stables which he also designed).

The first stone, containing one of the early coined sovereigns of William IV, was laid in October of that year and the building work, featuring exceptionally good masonry, was finished by 1836. The interior is spacious and elegant, with decoration restrained to chimney-pieces and ceilings. The principal rooms are grouped round the central hall which has a sensational staircase.

As designed by Dobson the balustrade of the staircase was wrought-iron, but between the wars the Cooksons commissioned Sir Edwin Lutyens to replace the metal with wood and also to prettify the walls with neo-Georgian plasterwork. Even an admirer of Lutyens must regret these unnecessary embellishments to Dobson's strikingly simple concept.

Since the death of Isaac Cookson in 1851, the estate has passed from father to eldest son. Isaac himself; his son John (who founded the Morpeth Hunt in 1854 and married one of the coal-owning Ridleys); his grandson, Philip (who married a sister of the 1st Lord Brassey of Apethorpe); and the present squire, Michael Cookson, have all served as High Sheriffs of Northumberland.

Michael Cookson, who is also a Deputy Lieutenant of the county, was born in 1927 and educated at Eton and Cirencester. He served in the East African Defence Forces and for 21 years with the Northumberland Hussars (later Queen's Own Yeomanry), achieving the rank of Brevet-Lieutenant-Colonel and the Territorial Decoration.

After farming one of the Duke of Northumberland's holdings near Hexham (and enjoying a couple of seasons as Joint-Master of the Heydon in the mid-1950s), Mr Cookson returned to Meldon in 1961, taking over the running of the place from his father, who now lives in the Mill House on the estate. He and his wife Romy (*née* Haggie) have three daughters and a son, James.

The Meldon estate now consists of some 5,000 acres, of which 2,000 are farmed in hand (two-thirds arable, one-third grass for ewes and cattle), 300 woodland and the rest let to five tenant farmers. Eleven people are employed on the estate. There is rough shooting, but hill drainage has put paid to the fishing.

In the last few years Mr Cookson has carried out major repair work to the house with the help of grant aid, including a new roof (at a cost of a six-figure sum), the replacement of lead gutters and the treatment of dry rot. Mr Cookson describes the opening of the house and the gardens (noted for their rhododendrons) as 'a loss leader' usually attracting some 1,500 visitors during the 30-day spring season. Mr Cookson says:

'If the people of this country wish houses such as Meldon to continue to exist as part of the heritage—especially when the occupants are of the family for whom the house was originally built—then more consideration must be paid to them financially to help to keep the system in being.'

'So often "the house", the centre-piece of the estate, was built in the middle of the property and through the ages parts of the estate have been sold and the rent roll diminished. Nowadays the financial drain to keep up the house and the immediate surroundings is a very large chunk out of one's income. And to do capital repairs, such as a new roof, in a great many instances the family is sacrificing itself for the sake of the family home.'

Opposite
Meldon: staircase hall.

Meldon Park, near Morpeth, Northumberland, is open to the public in the summer as advertised.

WILLIAMS OF CAERHAYS

Mr and Mrs Julian Williams.

Opposite
Caerhays Castle, Cornwall.

'LAST night I dreamt I went to Manderley again.' The evocative opening sentence of Daphne du Maurier's haunting novel *Rebecca* comes irresistibly to mind as one approaches Caerhays Castle, the seat of the Williams family on the south Cornish coast. In creating the fictional Manderley, Dame Daphne doubtless drew on several Cornish houses—above all Menabilly which she rented from the Rashleighs—but it was Caerhays that the BBC used as the location for the television dramatisation of *Rebecca* a few years ago.

The 60-acre Caerhays gardens, celebrated for their magnolias, *Williamsii* camellias and a profusion of horticultural treasures from Asia, were also featured on television in Roy Lancaster's series for Channel Four on the *Great Plant Collec-*

tions. The house itself is less well known though it is surely one of the best examples of a Nash castle and indeed a rare survivor of that undervalued species. Knepp Castle in Sussex (*see* page 000)—like several other Nash castles—was badly damaged by fire at the beginning of this century. The only other English survivor seems to be at Luscombe in Devon, home of the Hoares.

The fame of John Nash, who died in 1835, rests largely upon his architectural schemes for the Prince Regent, but his country houses made a significant contribution to the 'Picturesque' movement. At Caerhays, as the distinguished authority on Nash, Sir John Summerson, has pointed out, all their best qualities come together—dramatic silhouette, fine siting and magnificent landscape and gardens.

Here, too, are the familiar Nash features: a dominant circular tower; a *porte-cochère*; crudely over-simplified window tracery and finials; an absence of ornament and a purposeful asymmetry. Inside, there is one of Nash's special spinal galleries, rising to the roof and forming the basis of the ground plan for all downstairs and upstairs rooms which lead off it.

One of the reasons why so many of Nash's buildings have failed to survive until the present day is the notorious one that they were of technically unsound construction and therefore tended to subside or collapse. Another unfortunate characteristic of the great architect was the way his scant regard for economy resulted in ruin for his patrons.

The Caerhays commission was certainly no exception. Built from 1807 to 1808, of local granite and stone, the castle proved the undoing of the Trevanions. John Trevanion Purnell Bettesworth (later Trevanion), Whig MP for Penryn, overreached himself in building Caerhays and the family association with the estate, which had gone back to medieval times, eventually ended in 1840.

The poet Byron's grandmother was a Trevanion and in his book on *The Byrons and Trevanions*, A. L. Rowse relates how John Trevanion failed in his attempt to

Caerhays: garden view.

marry a rich widow, who would have restored the family fortunes, because his dog bit the lady's footman. The story goes that immediately before he went broke, Trevanion poignantly commissioned a painting showing the dog (a Chesapeake Bay retriever) on Caerhays Bay.

This vast canvas, now hanging in the present billiard room (added, like the old billiard room, in the 1890s) is the only memento of the Trevanions' long innings at Caerhays. By the time Michael Williams, Liberal MP for West Cornwall, bought the place in 1855, the castle was virtually derelict, without a roof or any of the original Nash furniture. A goose was apparently nesting in the fireplace of the circular drawing-room.

Michael Williams and his younger brother, Sir William Williams, 1st Baronet of Tregullow, were members of a Welsh mining dynasty who had migrated from Wales to Cornwall in the early 18th century. Thanks to Cornish tin, copper and a spot of banking, the Williamses were able to acquire several other West Country properties including Scorrier, Burncoose, Calstock, Gnaton and Werrington (bought in the 1880s for the rabbit shooting and now home of the present squire of Caerhays's elder brother).

Before his death in 1858, Michael Williams carried out a full-scale renovation of Caerhays Castle. He also shifted a large part of the hill behind Porthluney Cove, thereby opening up the glorious views of the castle that can be enjoyed from the coastal road.

The gardens began to take their present form in the mid-1890s when Michael's grandson, J. C. Williams, Liberal Unionist MP for Truro, decided to forsake the tedium of national politics and indulge his passion for horticulture. After initially concentrating on daffodils and bamboos, he experimented with Chinese rhododendrons and then raised the eponymous camellia hybrids from species sent back from China and Japan by such plant collectors as Ernest ('Chinese') Wilson and George Forrest.

A legendary figure in Cornwall, 'J. C.' had the then rare distinction for a commoner of being Lord Lieutenant of the county from 1918 to 1936. He was succeeded at Caerhays by his elder son, Charles, an MP for more than 30 years and Deputy Speaker of the House of Commons, where he upheld the democratic traditions in the Second World War by ensuring that there was some form of opposition to the government.

Caerhays: channel cut to improve the view; folly on the right.

At Caerhays his wartime contribution was to work tirelessly from dawn to dusk to prevent weeds and brambles from destroying the great garden. When not scything or Speakering, Charles stalked deer, amassing a record number of heads.

Charles's nephew, Julian Williams, who was president of the Cambridge Union in the generation of Geoffrey Howe and Patrick Jenkin, inherited Caerhays in 1955 shortly after being defeated as a Tory candidate in the general election of that year. The following year he married Delia Marshall, from St Mawes, who has done much to maintain Caerhays as a family home. Their two sons combine London careers with an interest in the Burncoose and Southdown Nurseries.

Over the last 30 years Julian Williams has enthusiastically upheld the family traditions of public service and preservation, serving his county as Deputy Lieutenant, Justice of the Peace, High Sheriff and chairman of the county council (sitting as an Independent).

At present the garden tends to be open for a few days every spring, but increased public access is being considered. The 3,500-acre estate is notable for the beautifully unspoilt coastline—the absence of tripperish impedimenta speaks volumes for private landownership.

The naming of the new plants in the garden reflects the cheerful atmosphere of the Caerhays community. A camellia is named after the late George Blandford, whose family have worked for the Williamses for more than a century and a rhododendron after Philip Tregunna, the head gardener. Another rhododendron is called after a less obliging character— Rebecca.

The gardens of Caerhays Castle, near Gorran, Cornwall, open in the spring as advertised.

CAPEL CURE
OF BLAKE HALL

Mr Ronald Capel Cure in front of a portrait of his father, Mr Nigel Capel Cure.

UNTIL very recently maps of the London Underground included a stop called 'Blake Hall' on the Central Line. The tube station may have gone but this eponymous family seat of the Capel Cures, a distinguished dynasty in the City of London, continues to adorn the rural hundred of Ongar in the much-maligned county of Essex.

Blake Hall is not far from Epping Forest, the remnant of a vast royal hunting ground. The manor in the parish of Bobbingworth (or 'Bovinger') passed through many hands over the centuries, including those of the Counts of Boulogne and of Eleanor of Castile. In 1709 it was purchased by John Clarke, whose daughter and heiress, Anne, married Sir Narbrough D'Aeth, 2nd Baronet, of Knowlton in Kent.

At the beginning of the 18th century Blake Hall was a typical timber-framed, gabled Essex building. This structure would appear to have been demolished in the early years of the Clarke ownership. The central rooms at the front of the present house (considerably extended in the 19th century) are part of the Georgian mansion which superseded the old manor house.

In 1789 Sir Narbrough D'Aeth, 3rd (and last) Baronet, a bachelor, sold Blake Hall to Capel Cure, a City merchant and member of Lloyd's. His descendant, Nigel Capel Cure, who served as Vice-Lord Lieutenant of Essex for 20 years and continued the family tradition in insurance, is the present Lord of the Manor.

The Cures had long been settled in Southwark where they practised the saddlery trade. Their founding father, Thomas Cure, whose will was proved in the year of the Armada, was saddler to Edward VI, Mary Tudor and Elizabeth I until succeeded by his son and namesake who served James I in a similar capacity. Although the exact connection has not been established it also seems likely that Thomas Cure was related to the celebrated royal sculptors of that time, Cornelius and William Cure.

Once settled in Essex, conveniently close to their business interests in the City, the Cures soon established themselves in the county. Capel Cure served as High Sheriff ten years after buying the Blake Hall estate which grew to nearly 4,000 acres in the 19th century.

From an estate map of 1804 it appears that Blake Hall was then a seven-bay, two-storey house with a colonnaded porch and a central pediment on the west (entrance) front. By this time the straight avenue of trees which had, in the late 18th century, led direct from the front door to the road had been abandoned in favour of curved approaches to the north and south.

Capel Cure died aged 70 in 1816 and was succeeded at Blake Hall by his son, George Capel Cure, who was responsible for the major changes to the house. First he called in the young classical architect George Basevi, junior (a cousin of Benjamin Disraeli's), who had recently been appointed surveyor of the newly formed Guardian Assurance Company.

Although it is recorded that Basevi was employed to remodel Blake Hall in 1822 it

is not clear how much work was actually done at that time. There are, however, two paintings by the artist Robert Cheney which show the west and east fronts at Blake Hall as they were in 1822.

Cheney, the star pupil of Peter de Wint, was the brother-in-law of George Capel Cure. Robert and his sister, Frederica Cheney, also a talented artist, came from the family that owned Badger Hall in Shropshire, a monumental house by James Wyatt (eventually sold by Nigel Capel Cure and later demolished).

It is known that a service wing to the north of Blake Hall was added in 1834, but the other additions—such as the third storey on the central block and the south wing—seem to have been made in about 1840. The fine late-17th-century staircase was installed in the early years of this century from Schomberg House in Pall Mall by the then squire, Major George Capel Cure.

The Major, a noted horseman and founder member of the Essex Hunt Club, was a nonagenarian, dying in 1943. The

Above
Blake Hall, Essex: west (entrance) front.

Blake Hall: staircase.

Right
Blake Hall: barn.

beautiful memorial of the Major and his wife, Ione (*née* Paley), in St Germain's Church, Bobbingworth, with its 16th-century Madonna and child attributed to Pietro Lombardo, was originally acquired from a palace in Mantua.

During the Second World War, Blake Hall was requisitioned by the Air Ministry which gutted the south wing and converted it into the Sector Operations Room of the North Weald Airfield. It was

Far right
Blake Hall: dining-room.

Right
Blake Hall: east (garden) front.

not until 1948 that Nigel Capel Cure was able to regain possession of the family seat—and its splendid cricket ground.

Mr Capel Cure, who served in the war with the Royal Artillery, was in the Eton cricket XIs of 1926 and 1927 and was later tried for Essex as well as being a first-class squash player. As High Sheriff of Essex his duties included proclaiming the accession of the present Queen in 1952, just as his forbear, George, had proclaimed William IV in 1830. His wife, Nancy (*née* Barry), was county president of the Essex

West Girl Guides for many years. Looking back from their present home across the park, they recall the enormity of their task in restoring the big house and its garden after the war.

Contemporary photographs certainly testify to an appallingly woebegone prospect: a monstrous red-brick extension, air-raid shelters, Nissen huts and so forth. Nearly 40 years on (not, incidentally, a phrase to strike a chord with this staunchly Etonian family), Blake Hall is now a flourishing showplace.

Recently Nigel's elder son, Ronald Capel Cure, a city director with C. T. Bowring and another keen all-round sportsman, moved into the big house. In 1982 he began opening the gardens regularly to the public. They are noted for their daffodils, narcissi, azaleas, rhododendrons and specimen trees and include the Ice House wood, a rose garden, a wild garden and a 'willow pattern' Japanese garden.

The old walled garden contains a garden centre; among the other popular attractions are a country and bird shop in the converted riding school, a model railway display and a tropical house full of

Blake Hall: Battle of Britain Museum in south wing.

butterflies. The south wing has recently been restored to its wartime state as the 'Ops Room' and is now a Battle of Britain museum.

For all its success in attracting the public Blake Hall itself emphatically remains the lived-in home of Ronald Capel Cure and his three sons. Ronald's wife Caroline (*née* Mills) died recently as the result of a riding accident.

In the best traditions of private land-ownership the 1,500-acre estate, as Ronald points out, is 'a small community in itself'. Owned by the same family for six generations, Blake Hall is a remarkable survival on the fringes of the metropolis.

Blake Hall gardens, Bovinger, near Ongar, Essex, are open daily as advertised.

FARQUHARSON OF BRAEMAR

Captain and Mrs Alwyne
Farquharson of Invercauld
(photographed at Invercauld House).

Captain and Mrs Alwyne
Farquharson of Invercauld
(photographed at Invercauld House).

SWATHED in tartan from head to foot, Captain Alwyne Farquharson, 16th Laird of Invercauld and his wife, Frances, epitomise the romance of the Higlands which they have done so much to foster through the annual festival at Braemar in Aberdeenshire. The programme of events, exhibitions, ceilidhs and other Caledonian jollifications culminates in the celebrated 'Gathering' of the Braemer Royal Highland Society.

Invercauld (or to give him his Gaelic style, *Mac Fhionnlaidh*) is a vice-patron of the Society which his family played a leading part in setting up in the 19th century. Now permanently settled at Princess Royal Park in the town of Braemar, the sites of previous games included the royal family's neighbouring Balmoral Castle and the Farquharsons' two seats, Invercauld House and Braemar Castle.

Unlike Invercauld House (the Farquharsons' principal seat, an impressive baronial pile greatly enlarged in the 19th century), Braemar Castle is open regularly to the public from May to early October to provide a romantic attraction to visitors to Deeside.

Braemar's story neatly embodies the turn and turn about of fate—and, for that matter, much modern Anglo-Scottish history. The castle was, in fact, first built by the Erskines in 1628 with a view to keeping their vassals and neighbours the Farquharsons in order.

The original castle was described by a contemporary as 'a great body of a house, a jam and a staircase'. In addition to fulfilling his need for a fortress on his Deeside estates from which to dominate the unruly Farquharsons, John Erskine, 2nd Earl of Mar, also found Braemar a handy hunting-lodge for the vast forests nearby. The estranged estates of the Earldom of Mar had been returned to his father by Mary Queen of Scots in 1565 and the Erskines were much exercised by the need to re-establish their pre-eminence.

At the time of the so-called 'Glorious Revolution', the 5th Earl of Mar was firmly on the side of 'Dutch William' (III) and consequently suffered at the hands of 'Bonnie Dundee' (John Grahame of Claverhouse) and his Jacobite followers. Among Bonnie Dundee's most colourful supporters was the formidable John Farquharson of Inverey, known as 'the Black Colonel'. This Laird of Inverey was not a man to meddle with; apparently he was in the habit of summoning his servants to the table by loosing off a pistol. In April 1689 he routed William III's Dragoons who were occupying Braemar Castle and set fire to the place so as to prevent it becoming a government garrison.

Ironically, this is exactly what it was to become nearly 60 years later in 1748 when the Black Colonel's kinsman, John Farquharson, the 9th Laird of Invercauld (who had purchased the neighbouring Braemar estate in 1732), decided to let the castle on a 99-year lease to the Hanoverian government at £14 per annum.

Lest is should be thought that this Farquharson was a faint heart, it should be noted that in his younger days the 9th Laird was 'out' in the 1715 Jacobite Rising. Doubtless his experience of languishing for almost a year in the notorious Marshalsea Prison as a result contributed to his refusal to come out again in the '45—though his daughter 'Colonel Anne' spunkily raised the Clan Chattan for Bonnie Prince Charlie when her husband, the 22nd Mackintosh of Mackintosh, decided, like his Farquharson father-in-law, to maintain a low profile. Displeased at the Farquharson's failure to join their cause, the Jacobite army plundered his Deeside estates. It is hardly surprising that he should have been minded to let Braemare become a garrison.

Opposite
Braemar Castle, Aberdeenshire.

Braemar: drawing-room.

In the second half of the 18th century the 10th Laird of Invercauld, an outstanding agriculturalist and forester, dedicated himself to the improvement and enlargement of his estates, while his wife, an Atholl Murray, encouraged the local flax-spinning industry. By the time of his death in 1805 the 10th Laird is said to have planted some 19 million trees.

Meanwhile, the army had vacated the garrison in the prematurely peaceful Aberdeenshire. Later in the 19th century the castle was restored as a family home by the 12th Laird whose mother, the only surviving child of the 10th Laird, had married a Ross but resumed the name of Farquharson. The 12th Laird's sister married the famous Scottish painter of portraits and sporting scenes, Sir Francis Grant.

Models in the red dining-room of the granite-built, harl-covered castle neatly illustrate the architectural history of Braemar from the fortress of the Erskines to the garrison of the Hanoverians to the seat of the Farquharsons. The battlemented star-shaped curtain wall and the topmost floors with their turrets constitute the main legacy of the rebuilding carried out from 1748 by the Board of Ordnance in Scotland. Their architect was John Adam, a brother of the great Robert.

The lower part of the castle remains basically the 2nd Earl of Mar's construction of 1628—a characteristically Scottish 'L'-shaped structure enfolding a round stair-tower. The front door is guarded by a massive 'yett', or iron gate.

Inside, the drawing-room, though now an attractive domesticated chamber decorated in pink and white, still recalls the castle's military past—the window shutters bear the graffiti of the Georgian soldiery, such as one Sergeant Chestnut who made his mark in 1779, the year the garrison packed its bags.

Other rooms on show include a third-floor bedroom with two semi-circular closets in the corner turrets; the morning room, containing the world's largest cairngorm (a gemstone); a vaulted room full of an assortment of stuffed creatures; and the old kitchens.

The enormous family estates of the Farquharsons of Invercauld were considerably reduced as a result of the extravagant tastes of the 13th Laird, known as 'Piccadilly Jim'. In 1874 this flashiest of Farquharsons found himself obliged to sell Ballochbuie Forest to Queen Victoria.

A 19th-century painting of the Braemar Games at the castle.

Even so, his engagingly modest great-grandson, the present Laird, must rank among the largest landowners in Scotland with property stretching for some 40 miles across Aberdeenshire and down to Perthshire.

It is difficult to estimate the acreage exactly as the estate includes much mountainous land but, excluding the hills, the present Laird puts it in the region of 120,000 acres. About 700 acres are farmed in hand (arable and 'policies'). To help make ends meet, most of the sport on the estate (deerstalking, shooting, and fishing on the Dee) is let and the Farquharsons also entertain paying guests mainly from overseas, at Invercauld House.

The present Laird was born a Compton of Newby in 1919 and succeeded his mother's sister, Myrtle, the 15th Lady of Invercauld, who was killed in the London blitz. He served with the Royal Scots Greys during the Second World War, winning the MC and being wounded in France in 1945

Four years later he married the American journalist and fashion editor Frances Lovell Oldham (formerly married to a Gordon and previously widow of a Rodney) and was also recognised by the Lord Lyon King of Arms as Chief of the Name of Farquharson and Head of the Clan.

The Farquharsons now divide their time between Invercauld, Braemar and the 12,000-acre Compton property on the Isle of Mull, Torloisk (his younger brother inherited the Newby estate in Yorkshire). The Laird is a JP for Aberdeenshire and sat on the county council for 26 years; he is also active in the British Deer Society, salmon trusts and the Scottish skiing industry.

His particular interest is forestry; without yet emulating the efforts of the improving 10th Laird the present Laird reckons he must have planted well over three million trees over the last 40 years. Another of his achievements was to install electricity and a proper water supply on the estate.

Once the open season at Braemar ends in October, the Farquharsons usually move back, frequently spending Christmas there. It says a lot for the Farquharsons of Invercauld, whose unassuming friendliness and love of tradition are bywords on Deeside, that this charming little castle should, after all its vicissitudes, remain a family home while providing so much public pleasure.

Braemar Castle, Braemar, Aberdeenshire, is regularly open to the public.

GODSAL OF ISCOYD

Above
Iscoyd Park, Clwyd: north and west fronts.

the scene is enhanced by a match in progress. Unfortunately, the day *The Field's* photographer called to capture the promised encounter between the local worthies and a visiting team from London, rain intervened, confining the flannelled Godsal menfolk to the new pavilion (opened by Richie Benaud in 1980).

Iscoyd's conscientious owner Philip Godsal, a chartered surveyor who heads the Shrewsbury office of John German, takes a special interest in rural housing. He is secretary of the Shropshire Rural Housing Association which seeks to provide housing for local people in the country at affordable rents. He is also deputy chairman of the Historic Houses Association for Wales and sits on the executive council of the HHA, as well as on the committee of the Shropshire branch of the Country Landowners Association.

Philip Godsal, born in 1945, was educated at Eton and before inheriting Iscoyd from his father a few years ago worked as a partner with Savills in East

ALTHOUGH the workaday professionals now tend to pack their bags early in September the cricket season is far from over for the true amateurs of the game. Country house cricket seems to be enjoying a revival and the mists of mellow fruitfulness surely lend extra enchantment to such exemplars of the Golden Age as Highclere (the Earl of Carnarvon), Ascott (Evelyn de Rothschild), Brympton d'Evercy (Charles Clive-Ponsonby-Fane), Torry Hill (Robin Leigh-Pemberton) and Everdon (Captain Dick Hawkins).

North Wales and the Welsh Marches are particularly well provided, with pitches at Marchwiel (the McAlpines) and Loton (Sir Michael Leighton, Bt—*see* PART I), as well as at Iscoyd Park, seat of the Godsal family, whose boundary virtually straddles the border between Shropshire and what was Flintshire.

The handsome Georgian red-brick house at Iscoyd looks at its best across the cricket ground in the park and doubtless

Right
Iscoyd Park: hall.

Iscoyd Park: library.

Anglia. During his sojourn in Suffolk he was evidently inspired by the pioneering example of one of his clients, Lord Henniker at Thornham, in alternative use for farm buildings that have been rendered redundant by the sheer size of modern machinery. Iscoyd is unusually rich in agricultural architecture (the outbuildings also include a handsome group of stables, coach-house and pigeon-house) and clearly there are considerable possibilities there.

Restoration of the outbuildings is proceeding with the help of grants from the Historic Buildings Council for Wales and Mr Godsal is currently submitting a planning application for change of use of some of the structures. The idea is to create a number of workshop units for letting, with the support of the Welsh Development Agency.

The house itself, which is listed Grade II*, has recently been substantially re-roofed, also with the help of an HBC grant. Inside there has been a sympathetic programme of redecoration. Mr Godsal's wife, Selina, stylishly manages the house, providing facilities for paying guests, private parties and conferences, as well as running her own flower-arranging business. Her particular interest, still in its early stages, is the creation of a new garden it Iscoyd.

The estate, never large (1,800 acres in 1900), is now about 750 acres, of which just fewer than half are farmed in hand in partnership. Mr Godsal has built up a small shoot (pheasants, duck and a few partridges) since returning from East Anglia, though he stresses that it hardly compares with the sport he used to enjoy there. The Sir Watkin Williams-Wynn

A meet of Sir Watkin Williams-Wynn's Hounds at Iscoyd, 1906.

Hunt meets regularly at Iscoyd and among its followers are Mrs Godsal's two elder daughters, Zoe and Lucinda. (Mrs Godsal has three girls by her previous marriage; Mr Godsal three sons and a daughter by his.)

The present house at Iscoyd is largely 18th-century, though there was obviously a dwelling on the site for several centuries before that. In the 14th century the estate was in the possession of the heirs of Iorweth Voel, Lord of Maelor Saesneg. Subsequently it passed by marriage to the Roydens of Holt. In the 17th century the Jennings family lived there and in 1737 William Hanmer, who had married the Jennings heiress of Gopsal, Leicestershire, proceeded to build the front part of the house.

Hanmer, scion of a long-established Flintshire family, had been obliged to leave his own family seat of Fenns nearby because the water supply failed. It is not clear exactly what was there before he began building operations at Iscoyd but the existing structure probably included the library wing. Judging from the position of the timbers and the brickwork it appears that this attractive wing was once only two storeys high, with a double-pitched roof.

The style of the library—Iscoyd's most remarkable interior, with an exquisite Venetian window—looks earlier than 1737 and it seems an unusually grand room considering the size of that wing. It

seems likely it was formerly larger and part of it was demolished.

Hanmer's daughter and heiress, Esther, married the first Viscount Curzon (ancestor of the present Earl Howe) and Iscoyd was sold in 1780 to the Reverend Richard Congreve, of Congreve, Staffordshire (cousin of William, the dramatist). The squarson's spinster daughter, Marianne, then sold it in 1843 to Philip Lake Godsal, son of an enterprising coach-maker, art collector and financial wheeler-dealer from Cheltenham.

P. L. Godsal, who married the elder daughter of the 1st Lord Wynford, the Victorian judge, added the portico and the dining-room. His son, Philip William Godsal, was responsible for the bow to the drawing-room in 1876.

P. W. Godsal was an improving agriculturalist and rural philanthropist who believed that his tenants should have the opportunity of farming their own smallholdings. His wife, Charlotte Garth, was the heiress of Haines Hill, Berkshire, one of England's finest 'unknown' houses and now the seat of Philip Godsal's cousin Alan Godsal.

The heir to Iscoyd, Major Philip Thomas Godsal, applied sound military principles to the writing of Roman history in *The Conquest of Ceawlin*. An outstanding shot, he was a founder member of the English Eight Club in 1878. His inventions included the celebrated Godsal rifle which was nearly adopted by the Army

elegant glazing bars.

The good work has been faithfully carried on by his son and successor. From the majestic elegance of the library to the atmospheric gun-room, this is a family seat of satisfying quality. It is reassuring to learn from Philip Godsal that its future has been secured in accordance with the proper heritage procedures and it is pleasing to report that his eldest son, Philip Langley Godsal, who is a schoolboy at Shrewsbury and takes a keen interest in the estate, looks set to become in due course the seventh Philip Godsal of Iscoyd.

As for cricket, weather permitting, the Iscoyd wicket is normally in use twice a week, thus playing its part in forging the traditional links between country houses and the local community.

Iscoyd Park, near Whit-church, Shropshire, is open to the public by written appointment.

Left
Iscoyd Park: dovecote.

Below
Mr Philip Godsal and his sons, Benjamin (left) and Thomas.

instead of the Lee-Enfield. The eccentric tower at Iscoyd, ingeniously designed to house the water tanks and a battery of bathrooms, was one of his contributions.

What one sees today at Iscoyd, so well-ordered and so pleasantly disposed, is all the more remarkable when one considers what the place was like 30 years ago. For during the Second World War, after a genteel interlude as the outpost of St Godric's Secretarial College, Iscoyd was requisitioned for use as a 1,500-bed hospital for the United States Forces, with a prisoner-of-war camp in the enclosure. The beautiful parkland was obliterated by an Orwellian nightmare of Nissen huts, barbed wire and control towers. Eventually the Americans handed over the camp to some displaced persons in the shape of Polish refugees.

Philip Godsal's grandfather, Major Philip Godsal (who won the Military Cross in the First World War and was land agent to Sir Watkin Williams-Wynn), returned to the house in 1946, but because of the continuing presence of the camp, lived in a self-contained flat on the first floor in the library wing. It was not until 1957 that the park was finally restored to the family and the Poles moved to join their compatriots at a nearby camp.

In the 1960s Major Philip Hugh Godsal (the present owner's father) brought the main rooms of the house back into use and restored the Georgian facade, replacing the Victorian plate-glass windows with

LEFROY OF CARRIGGLAS

Above
Mr and Mrs Jeffry Lefroy and their two sons.

Far right
Carrigglas Manor, Co Longford: entrance to farmyard.

Right
Carrigglas Manor: drawing-room.

(*see* PART IV). Similarly, at Carrigglas Manor in Co Longford, seat of the Lefroy family, the Tudor-Gothic Revival pile—exceptional though it is—takes second place to the magnificent Georgian stables.

Originally a Jacobean manor of the Bishops of Ardagh, Carrigglas (or Carrickglass, as it was then known) was bequeathed in the 17th century to Trinity College, Dublin. In the 18th century

RACE meetings serve as constant reminders of the relative importance of horses and humans. Not only on the Turf do the animals enjoy the upper hand; architecturally the stables can sometimes be finer than the mansion house. This is the case, for instance, at Althorp and at Peover Hall in Cheshire

Trinity leased it to the Newcomen family. The stables were built in the 1790s for Sir William Gleadowe-Newcomen, Bt, a Dublin banker and MP for the county of Longford.

Sir William's architect was James Gandon, an Englishman of Huguenot descent and a former pupil of Sir William Chambers, who became Dublin's most distinguished neo-classical designer. In his recent definitive study of *James Gandon: Vitruvius Hibernicus*, Edward McParland, who lectures on the History of Art at Trinity College, Dublin, observes that the startling entrance to the Carrigglas farmyard 'speaks of a stern primitivism, an interest in abstraction, and an expressive combination of delicacy and power which makes this fragment of a *barrière* remarkable in any context'.

Gandon's outbuildings extend round two courtyards with pedimented and rusticated archways. An imposingly elegant pedimented archway leads to the stables. Gandon also designed the entrance gateway to the park.

Sadly, his plans for a new house at Carrigglas for Sir William Gleadowe-Newcomen were never executed. They survive in the National Library of Ireland showing a noble, domed, pedimented and porticoed villa echoing the Roman Pantheon.

Sir William had married the heiress of the Carrigglas tenancy, Charlotte Newcomen, in about 1770, and was created a Baronet in 1781. In 'consideration of her husband's services'—in other words, for supporting the Act of Union with Great

Above
Carrigglas: entrance front.

Carrigglas: staircase hall.

Carrigglas: dining-room.

Carrigglas: entrance to stableyard.

Britain in return for an alleged cash payment of £10,000—Charlotte was created a Baroness and then a Viscountess. Richard Lovell Edgeworth, the father of Maria the novelist, poured poetic scorn:

With a name that is borrowed—a title
                    that's bought,
Sir William would fain be a gentleman
                    thought;
His wit is but cunning, his courage but
                    vapour,
His pride is but money—his money but
                    paper!

These lines proved prophetic for Newcomen's Bank duly went bust. Sir William's son and successor, the 2nd Viscount Newcomen, was said to have lived alone in the bank 'gloating ... over ingots of treasure, with no lamp to guide him but the luminous diamonds which had been left for safe-keeping in his hands'. Wrapped in a sullen misanthropy he was sometimes seen 'emerging at twilight from his iron-clamped abode'. He finally shot himself in 1825 when the bank stopped payment.

Meanwhile the lease of Carrigglas had been taken up by an alumnus of Trinity, Thomas Langlois Lefroy, a Dublin barrister of Huguenot descent whose father, a Cavalry colonel, had been quartered and settled in Ireland since 1770. The Lefroys, originally from Cambrai, provide a reminder that by no means all the 'Ascendancy' were of 'Anglo' background; La Touche and Le Fanu are other examples of distinguished Huguenot Irish dynasties.

Although Thomas Lefroy went on to become an MP, a Baron of the Exchequer and Chief Justice, his chief claim to fame rests upon his intimacy with Jane Austen. 'He is a very gentlemanlike, good-looking pleasant young man,' Jane assured her sister Cassandra. Their flirtatious friendship certainly raised expectations of a betrothal in the Hampshire of the mid-1790s. In old age the Chief Justice recalled his feelings for Jane as 'a boyish love'.

Lefroy, who sat with his son Anthony (MP for Longford) in the Reform Parliament, eventually bought the freehold of the Carrigglas estate. In 1873 he fulfilled his ambition of pulling down the rambling old manor house in order to replace it with an impressive structure in the latest style. Tom placed the matter in the hands of the Almighty ('But Thine the work, the Blessing Thine') and the architect Daniel Robertson of Kilkenny. Building operations continued until 1840, resulting in a cluster of gables, oriels and polygonal battlemented turrets.

Inside, the drawing-room ceiling was adorned with plaster Gothic ribs and a multicoloured cornice of foliage. There is more foliage in the cornices of the library and the dining-room, though there the ceiling is Tudorish. The library has Gothic bookcases; the staircase, lit by a stained glass window, has cast-iron balustrades.

The remarkable interiors have recently been sympathetically redecorated by

Carrigglas: costumes.

Tom's great-great-great-grandson, Jeffry Lefroy, and his wife, Tessa (*née* White). Carrigglas now appears on the Historic Irish Tourist Houses and Gardens Association list of places open regularly to the public.

The attractions include Mrs Lefroy's imaginative arrangements of period costumes. She is also reviving the woodland garden and creating a new formal garden. In addition to these activities she writes articles and is currently working on a biography of her late uncle, Sir Thomas Monnington, a former president of the Royal Academy. The Lefroys have two sons, Langlois and Edward.

Mr Lefroy maintains the Huguenot traditions of his family as a director of La Providence, the French Hospital. He was a noted Balliol oarsman—and well deserves his billing as 'the best bath baritone in Ireland'. He served in the Royal Irish Fusiliers and retired some 10 years ago to farm. He is a director of the Irish Landowners' Convention and represented Co Longford on the General Council of the Committee of Agriculture in Dublin. He is a forestry contractor and a former secretary of the Irish Timber Growers' Association. There are now 130 acres of hardwoods and 55 acres of conifers at Carrigglas.

Mr Lefroy took over Carrigglas from a cousin, Phoebe Lefroy. Miss Lefroy, a talented artist, did much to revive the estate and still farms part of the land. In previous generations the place had become run down. Lieutenant-Colonel Hugh Lefroy (died 1954) was an eccentric, if often brilliant, inventor who grew potatoes on the roof and pruned the apple trees by night so as to cause least distress to the trees. His striking Polish wife, Helen, had a mission to convert the Roman Catholics of Longford to Protestantism, but had more success in setting up the local district nursing service.

Today Carrigglas Manor is one of the only two surviving family seats in Co Longford (Castle Forbes, seat of the Earl of Granard, is the other) whereas a century ago there were 42. Therefore the Lefroys' enthusiastic determination to keep the place going is especially admirable. Their main project at the moment is the restoration of Gandon's stables in which they intend to house a museum, a shop, a tea-room and some holiday apartments—principally for fishermen.

Horses, however, will still predominate. The Lefroys bred the Irish Army's Olympic hope, Cairn Hill, a recent winner of the Tidworth and Tweseldown events and supreme champion at the 1984 Royal Dublin Horse Show. Another horse bred at Carrigglas was the showjumper Darcy, whose name recalls one great writer the Irish narrowly missed calling their own.

Carrigglas Manor, near Longford, Co Longford, is open to the public as advertised.

LOWRY OF BLESSINGBOURNE

Captain and Mrs Robert Lowry.

NORTHERN Ireland now contains some 50 extant family seats. The cheerful and peaceful reality of these estates and their dependent communities is certainly far removed from the images of Ulster projected on the television screen.

Indeed, for those who know better than to believe what they are told by the media Northern Ireland is still a pleasant place in which to take a holiday. It is not so crowded as Scotland and offers scenery and sport no less memorable.

Among the family seats offering hospitality, sport and entertainment is Blessingbourne near Fivemiletown, Co Tyrone, in the Clogher Valley, where Robert and Angela Lowry have stylishly converted the stable block into holiday apartments. There is more accommodation in a house within the walled garden, coarse fishing on the lough and burgeoning museums in the farm buildings featuring a noted collection of coaches and carriages, cos-

Opposite
Blessingbourne, Co Tyrone: garden front across lake.

128

Blessingbourne: hall.

The Montgomerys were another Lowland Scots family, Ayrshire cadets of the Lords Montgomerie (later Earls of Eglington and Winton), who received grants of land in Ulster in the early 17th century. Hugh Montgomery, a Captain of Horse in William III's Army, acquired Derrygonnelly Castle in Co Fermanagh through marriage to the Derrygonnelly heiress Katherine Dunbar.

Their son, another Hugh, added the Blessingbourne lands to the family holdings in the early 18th century through his marriage to Elizabeth Armar, daughter of the Archdeacon of Connor, but there was no house there at this stage. Derrygonnelly Castle was burnt later in the 18th century and not rebuilt.

The next Hugh, who married a daughter of the 1st Viscount Gosford, rented Castle Hume, Co Fermanagh (Richard Castle's first Irish Palladian house) for a spell. Their son, painted by Archer-Shee in his 15th Dragoons uniform as his Eton leaving portrait and later Lieutenant-Colonel of the Fermanagh Militia, was known as 'Colonel Eclipse'.

Crossed in love (the object of his passion, Anna Maria Dashwood proceeded to marry the 2nd Marquess of Ely, the owner of Castle Hume), Colonel Eclipse vowed never to marry. He decided to build a snug bachelor retreat for himself and chose a delightful spot beside the lough at Blessingbourne with a glorious view of the Monaghan mountains for a romantic thatched cottage. Some years later, however, on a tour of Spain his resolve failed and in 1821 he married Senorita Maria Dolores Plink from Malaga.

For the next 50 years the family lived mainly abroad so the cottage at Blessingbourne was all they needed for their

tumes, household impedimenta and old agricultural implements.

The enterprising Captain Lowry, a Deputy Lieutenant for Co Tyrone and former chairman of the local diary co-operative, took over the running of the Blessingbourne estate in the mid-1960s after retiring from the Royal Irish Fusiliers. He and his wife, Angela (*née* Woods), who has worked tirelessly to rescue the garden and maintain the imposing Tudor Revival house, have two sons and a daughter. The children began their education in the primary school (inter-denominational let it be noted) built by Captain Lowry's maternal great-grand-father on the estate.

In the male line Captain Lowry belongs to a junior branch of the Earl of Belmore's family who settled, like so many Lowland Scots, in Ulster in the 17th century. This line of Lowrys was formerly seated at Pomeroy House, Co Tyrone (now demol-ished, having been sold to the Forestry Commission), and also owned the Agh-nablaney estate in Co Fermanagh. Robert is the only son of the late Commander Graham Lowry of Glasdrumman House, Co Down, who enjoyed the distinction of being in action as a midshipman of 15 whereas his own father, Admiral Sir Rob-ert Lowry, had never seen a shot fired in anger during 40 years in the Navy.

The Commander married Mary, or 'Molly', Montgomery, the eldest daugh-ter of Major-General Hugh Montgomery, the owner of Blessingbourne. This estate was eventually made over to Robert Lowry by his bachelor uncle, Peter Mont-gomery, the conductor and former presi-dent of the Arts Council of Northern Ireland.

Blessingbourne: dining-room.

occasional visits to their estates in Co Tyrone and Co Fermanagh. This exile was not caused by 'absenteeism' but poor health. Colonel Eclipse's son, Hugh the sixth, lived at Hofwyl in Switzerland, the home of his wife, Maria de Fellenberg, daughter of the Landamann of Berne.

The present Victorian-Elizabethan mansion at Blessingbourne was built from 1870 to 1874 by Hugh de Fellenberg Montgomery to the designs of his friend Frederick Pepys Cockerell, who was later to build Clonalis House, Co Roscommon, for the O'Conor Don [see PART I].

Cockerell, an artist as well as an architect, was the son of the great neo-classicist C. R. Cockerell, but was of a more romantic persuasion than his father. His first design for Blessingbourne featured a fantastic *porte-cochère* but unfortunately this was rejected on grounds of cost. A modest, conscientious squire, H. de F. Montgomery wanted his new house to be built out of income rather than capital though in the

event he had to raise extra cash to cover Cockerell's undertaking.

The result has been described as one of the finest pieces of Tudor· Revival in Ireland. Even those who do not normally care for that sort of architecture have to concede that this is an unusually attractive example of its style and period. As Mark Bence-Jones has pointed out in his *Country Houses of Ireland*: 'The grey stone elevations are not over-loaded with ornament; such as there is has restraint: caps on the chimneys, small finials on the gables, curved and scrolled pediments over some of the mullioned windows.'

The comfortable interior is full of character. The hall has a staircase incorporated in a screen of tapering wooden piers. The Tudorish chimneypieces, some adorned with de Morgan tiles, are flanked by niches for logs and turf. There are original William Morris wallpapers in the dining-room and the library; the drawing-room was done up in the 1960s by Peter Montgomery.

The credit for Blessingbourne was due just as much to the patron as to the architect. Hugh de Fellenberg Montgomery and his wife, Mary Maude, a granddaughter of the 1st Viscount Hawarden, were people of taste who gave the house an atmosphere all of its own. Mary founded the local copper industry and H. de F. was the most benevolent of landlords.

An account of his liberal stewardship of the then 14,000-acre family estate is given in Patrick Buckland's study of *Ulster Unionism*. He ended up as 'Father' of the Senate of the new Parliament of Northern Ireland at Stormont and became a Privy Councillor in 1924, but turned down a baronetcy. He was succeeded at Blessingbourne by his eldest son, yet another Hugh, who was one of the many modern generals to be produced by Ulster.

'The General', as he was always known, was, however, for removed from the traditional picture of a military man. Highly individual and unstuffy, he was at his happiest with his scout troop or tracking down medieval stained glass. Always a doughty opponent of bigotry, he worked hard for harmony in Northern Ireland and founded the Irish Association which sought to ensure that communal activities transcended religious differences.

These ideals were faithfully pursued by his second son Peter, a figure of immense charm, who succeeded the General at Blessingbourne in 1954. A pioneering champion of the arts in Northerm Ireland, he founded the Fivemiletown Choral Society and the Ulster Orchestra, and in his younger days used to conduct the BBC Northern Ireland Orchestra. His numerous appointments included the chairmanship of the Board of Visitors to Belfast prison and he was Vice-Lieutenant of Co Tyrone until ill-health obliged him to retire from public affairs in 1979.

Happily, by that time the Lowrys were well advanced in their admirable efforts to give Blessingbourne a new lease of life.

Blessingbourne, Five-miletown, Co Tyrone, is not open to the public though local events are held regularly and holiday apartments are available for letting.

Blessingbourne: drawing-room.

HOBHOUSE
OF HADSPEN

Mr and Mrs Paul Hobhouse.

IT IS a curious anomaly that while the National Trust membership runs to well over a million, the Friends of the Historic Houses Association, the body that champions the privately-owned heritage, number only a few thousand. The benefits of being a Friend of the HHA include free admission to nearly 300 HHA houses open to the public and also the occasional opportunity to see round houses not normally open such as, for instance, the exceptionally pleasing and intimate Hadspen House in Somerset, seat of the Hobhouses for the last 200 years.

Once part of the holdings of the Dukes of Somerset, Hadspen was bought in the 1680s by William Player, a lawyer from London putting together a country estate round Castle Cary. At that stage there was a gabled farmhouse on the site known as Byfleet Close. Player recorded that in 1687 he 'Built the forefront of a Gentleman's House in Byfleet Close'.

According to Andrew Raven, who has made a scholarly study of the house's architecture, it seems that 300 years ago the principal facade may have been basically as it appears today. The exceptions would have been the windows, then still mullioned and transomed rather than sash—and also lower on the first floor—and the pediment, which then contained an *oeil de boeuf*.

Although Sir Nikolaus Pevsner observed that the facade looks about 1750 to 1770, Mr Raven argues that the metropolitan Player would surely have had some knowledge of classical developments. The only difficult craftsmanship for Somerset masons in the new architectural vocabulary was the sash window. Tintinhull Manor nearby (now owned by the National Trust) provides a more or less contemporary example of a classical facade with mullioned and transomed windows.

In the 18th century the stone mullioned and transomed windows were removed to the stables by Vickris Dickinson, who bought Hadspen from the trustees of Player's son. The Dickinsons, like their relations the Pinneys of Bettiscombe [*see* PART IV], and many other West Country squires, owed their fortune to Bristol—or, in other words, the slave trade.

In her engaging book *Winging Westward*, Joy Burden (a descendant of Vickris's brother, Caleb, who bought Kingweston House a couple of years earlier) says that when she met Paul Hobhouse, the present occupant of Hadspen, she 'considered a Dickinson apology due' for the label on the weathervane of the Hadspen stables. It reads: 'VD 1747'.

Dickinson duly installed sash windows in the main house and made various improvements about the place. In her diary of a journey to Cornwall in 1759, Mariabella Eliot noted 'the sight of a very handsome house, low and wide, regularly built with a yellowish sort of stone, before which was a very long and wide lawn . . .'.

Seven years later Hadspen was put on the market. The advertisement in the *Lloyds Evening Post* for 13/15 October 1766 refers to the woods preserving 'a great deal of game' and, perhaps significantly, to 'a *modern* Stone built House . . .' (my italics). The responsibility for Hadspen's main facade, to the south, ultimately remains unproven.

Most of the later changes and additions are, however, well-documented. Henry Hobhouse QC, the head of the Bristol Bar (who purchased the estate for £19,500 in 1785 after it had gone through two other ownerships since the departure of the Dickinsons) remodelled the interior and added the flamboyantly 'Adamesque' dining-room on the east front. The height of the drawing-room and the library (the two front rooms probably created by Hobhouse's predecessor John Ford) was also raised. Engravings and paintings by the QC's spinster daughter, Sarah, show the rationalised, four-square result in about 1805.

The present entrance porch was added to the west in 1886 by Henry Hobhouse, MP. To accommodate his growing family (seven children, of whom six survived) he built the north-west wing in 1900 and the south-east, or garden, wing nine years later. The former extension is carefully

'Georgian'; the latter, with its colonnade, represents a bolder adaptation of classical motifs.

The Hobhouses, originally master mariners from Minehead, also made their money in Bristol out of slavery. As if to atone for this they later tended to eschew 'trade' and became Liberals, philanthropists and public servants. Paul Hobhouse corrects the romantic notion put forward in one family memoir that they have constituted 'a long line of Somerset squires'. In fact, for the most part, the family has been away in the world of public affairs; indeed Mr Hobhouse himself is the first incumbent of Hadspen to be really based upon the land.

The QC's son and namesake was Under-Secretary of State at the Home Office when he suffered the embarrassment of seeing his radical cousin John Cam Hobhouse, Byron's great friend, committed to Newgate. Later John Cam became a highly respectable politician and ended as president of the Board of Control and a peer.

The Under-Secretary went on to

Hadspen House, Somerset: south front.

Hadspen House: dining-room.

become Keeper of State Papers and a Privy Councillor. His descendants have included Arthur, the 1st and last Lord Hobhouse, a particular benefactor of Hadspen; a bishop and a brace of archdeacons; a judge and various other lawyers, physicians, professors and social reformers, such as Leonard Hobhouse, one of the founding fathers of the London School of Economics. The present generation includes the publisher Caroline Hobhouse and the eminent conservationist Hermione Hobhouse, the editor of the *Survey of London* and former secretary of the Victorian Society.

The Henry Hobhouse who extended Hadspen at the turn of the century was also a Privy Councillor, a leading layman in the Church and the first chairman of the Somerset County Council. His wife, Margaret Potter, was the sister of the formidable Fabian do-gooder Beatrice Webb—and thus an aunt of Malcolm Muggeridge's wife, Kitty, who used to come to Hadspen when she was at school nearby in Bruton.

When Margaret arrived at Hadspen in 1880 the house stood in a field with sheep grazing up to the windows. There was, however, an 18th-century walled garden, an orchard, an avenue of elms (destroyed by the deleterious disease of 1976), a reservoir, a gardener's cottage and stone-built kennels for a pack of harriers. From

Hadspen House: garden pool.

den to mature into a paradise of colour and form. Mr Hobhouse points out that, although the eight-acre garden is more than 400 feet above sea-level, the wonderfully favourable 'micro-climate' provides shelter for a multitude of tender plants.

Mr Hobhouse, who was born in 1927, educated at Eton and Trinity College, Cambridge, and served in the Life Guards, had formerly lived on Colonsay. He still farms some 4,000 acres rented from Lord Strathcona up there with his younger son, David, and his daughter Georgina; the elder son, Niall, runs the Hobhouse art gallery in Duke Street. The family sheep enterprise on Colonsay is tied in with that at Hadspen, where some 650 acres of the estate are farmed in hand (principally dairy and corn).

Mr Hobhouse's elder brother Henry (but known as 'Tom') also farms nearby, as does his own son, the ninth Henry Hobhouse, a well-known West Country organic agriculturalist. Tom published (under his baptismal name) the widely acclaimed *Seeds of Change*, a remarkably original book it shows the hitherto unconsidered effect of sugar, tea, quinine, cotton and the potato on the course of history. He is now working on a sequel about the staples of the ancient world: corn, oil and wine.

Paul Hobhouse is married to the art historian Jeannie Chapel. She is an authority on 19th-century patronage and is the co-author of *The Fine and Decorative Art Collections of Britain and Ireland* produced for the National Art Collections Fund. Mrs Hobhouse has a particular affection for the evocative walled garden (with its Hosta Walk leading down to the Lutyens seat) and the outbuildings at Hadspen. They are indeed enchanting and quintessentially Somerset.

this nucleus the Hobhouses of Hadspen have created, during the last century, one of the most delightful and interesting gardens in England.

As well as erecting the stone terraces to exclude the sheep, Margaret enriched the new garden with ornaments, seats and statues (including two nudes banished from the dining-room by her prudish stepmother-in-law) and planted many fine trees and shrubs. Following the death in 1965 of her son, Sir Arthur Hobhouse, chairman of numerous government reports (notably the one recommending the setting up of National Parks), came the garden's glorious renaissance.

Much of the credit for this must go to Paul Hobhouse's first wife, Penelope (*née* Chichester-Clark), the celebrated gardening writer, whose artistic eye and knowledge of plants enabled the restored gar-

Hadspen House, near Castle Cary, Somerset, is not open to the public, but the gardens and nursery are open all year (except January), as advertised.

PHILLIPS OF WOMBOURNE WODEHOUSE

Mr and Mrs John Phillips, with the north front of The Wombourne Wodehouse, Staffordshire, in the background.

THE CONNECTION between the great composer George Frederick Handel and the cheerful 1930s musical *Me and My Girl*, still packing them in at the Adelphi Theatre in the Strand, might well seem slight. It is. Nonetheless, a link can be traced through The Wombourne Wodehouse in Staffordshire, home of Mr and Mrs John Phillips. The Wodehouse once belonged to Handel's friend and devoted fan, Sir Samuel Hellier, the musicologist, and has lately been the location for two Central Television comedy series: *Mog* (featuring Enn Reitel, star of *Me and My Girl*) and *The Other 'Arf* (with John Standing and Lorraine Chase, herself the leading lady of the jolly 'Lambeth Walk' musical).

Certain connoisseurs of lesser-known country houses have faithfully sat through these mildly excruciating programmes—the one set in a loony-bin, the other in a 'state'—so as to enjoy the odd glimpse of a particularly interesting and unusual building. The Wodehouse's architectural history has included such intriguing names as James Gandon, G. F. Bodley and that master of the arts and crafts, C. R. Ashbee.

There seems to have been a house on the site at least since the 13th century.

Formerly known as Woodhouse (the present archaic spelling was adopted, as one might expect, in the High Victorian period), the core of the present house is a late-medieval timber-framed structure of which the hall and parlour-end survive. The Wodehouse Bedroom, above the present hall, has an impressive spere truss.

Until the beginning of the 18th century Woodhouse was the seat of the Woodhouse family. Gabled wings had been added by the mid-17th century and in 1666 the house was assessed at 'six hearths'. The first of the family to style himself 'gent', Edward Wodehouse, died in 1688 leaving his estate encumbered with mortgages. By that stage the property consisted of two parlours, a hall, a kitchen, a brewhouse, a bakehouse, two butteries, a dairy and a pantry, with eight chambers on the first floor.

More mortgages were to follow in the 1690s. Then in 1703 the mortgagees, who included a connection of the Woodhouses', Rupert Huntbatch, began the inexorable foreclosure proceedings. By 1708 Woodhouse was in the ownership of Huntbatch's son-in-law, Samuel Hellier, a London brewer. In the 1740s Hellier's son and namesake carried out some extensive modernisation to the interiors, such as the installation of panelling and a new staircase within the medieval parlour.

It was said of the third Samuel Hellier, who succeeded to the estate in 1751 at the age of 15, that he had 'no vice . . . but the love of music'. A keen violinist and collector of musical instruments, while he was still an undergraduate at Oxford he befriended Handel and began buying the elderly composer's manuscript scores in 1756.

In memory of his Hanoverian hero, Hellier commissioned James Gandon, the architect best known for his work in Ireland [*see* Carrigglas Manor, page 124], to design a classical temple at Woodhouse in 1768. This was one of a variety of fantastic buildings erected in the pleasure-grounds; the others included an octagon, a root house, a grotto, a druids' temple, a hermitage (complete

Wodehouse: drawing-room.

with several rooms and a life-size model of a hermit known as 'Father Francis') and, of course, a music room equipped with an organ.

The place became a popular attraction—though rather too popular for Hellier's taste. To exclude what he called 'tag, rag and rabble', only 'such who came in coaches and appear as people of fashion' were admitted. Sadly none of the garden buildings has survived; though a lake (recorded there in 1710) still adorns a remarkably rural scene only a few miles from the centre of Wolverhampton.

Samuel Hellier served as High Sheriff of Worcestershire in 1762 and was

Wodehouse: south (entrance) front.

Wodehouse: hall.

knighted the same year when he presented the county's loyal address to George III on the birth of the Prince of Wales. On his death in 1784 Sir Samuel, a bachelor, left all his property to his friend, the Reverend Thomas Shaw, a local parson.

In this case Shaw (who duly took the additional surname of Hellier) had acted as Sir Samuel's 'man of business' and doubtless helped to restrain some of his more extravagant flights of fancy. Among unexecuted plans for the remodelling of Woodhouse during Sir Samuel's ownership were works by such architects as his friend Gandon, William Baker of Highfields and Joseph Pickford of Derby.

That is not to say Shaw-Hellier himself was lacking in architectural schemes. John Plaw, the architect of Belle Isle on Lake Windermere, published designs for a neoclassical villa on the site of the existing house in 1800. In the event, Shaw-Hellier added the drawing-room and dining-room to the north front and replaced the straight gables by a Jacobean roofline of tall chimneys and Flemish gables.

The next changes came during the ownership of the fortunate clergyman's great-grandson Colonel Thomas Shaw-Hellier, who succeeded his father, the Master of Albrighton known as 'Huntsman Hellier', in 1870. First, in the early 1870s, Bodley remodelled the south and west fronts, again in 'Jacobean' manner and added a porch and square bay windows. He also heightened and redecorated the drawing-room.

Then in the 1890s Ashbee, a former pupil of Bodley's, arrived to give the gables a faint look of his beloved Monta-

cute. He replaced two of the gables by a parapet with the motto *DOMUM DULCE DOMUM* (his client, the Colonel, was a Wykehamist). He was also responsible for building the surprisingly 'Dutch'-style chapel and the billiard room to the east.

Among the other work carried out for the Colonel was another music room—this time in part of the stables (a principally 19th-century block which incorporated a coach-house of 1743). The Colonel was commandant of the Royal Military School of Music at Kneller Hall.

Like his great-grandfather's benefactor and fellow-musicologist, the somewhat eccentric and High Church Colonel was a

Wodehouse: west front.

Far left
Wodehouse: bedroom with spere truss.

bachelor by temperament. His marriage late in life to the owner of the neighbouring Lloyd estate, Harriet Bradney-Marsh, was not a success. Soon afterwards he emigrated to Sicily where Ashbee had designed him a villa at Taormina.

The Wodehouse (as it was now known) then passed to the Colonel's nephew, Evelyn Simpson, of the Baldock brewing family, who was married to another cousin, Fanny Phillips, of the Stamford brewing family. They took the surname of Shaw-Hellier and, in 1912, added an extensive service wing to the east. Ashbee's chapel and billiard-room were sub-divided to form smaller rooms.

After the death in action of their only son, Arthur Shaw-Hellier, at Gallipoli in 1915, time rather stood still at the Wodehouse. The place was inherited by Arthur's spinster sisters, Molly (a racehorse owner and enthusiastic Gun) and Dorothy. After Dorothy's death her first

cousin twice removed, John Phillips, came into the property.

Born in 1935 and educated at Bryanston and Cirencester, Mr Phillips married Carolyn Grylls and they have a son and a daughter. About two-thirds of the arable land on the 800-acre estate is farmed in hand. The major restoration in recent years has included rewiring, new plumbing, the attractive lightening of the yew panelling, cleaning of 'pickled' family portraits and the felling of some 40 trees to open up the brook in the well-wooded grounds.

Apart from its occasional use as a television location, Wodehouse is also the setting for numerous charitable events and,

Far left
Wodehouse: bedroom with spere truss.

Below
Wodehouse: stables.

suitably enough in view of its musical past, for concerts. In the words from the 'Lambeth Walk', which Miss Chase enunciates in her prize Cockney: 'Why don't you make your way there, Go there . . .'.

The Wombourne Wodehouse, Wolverhampton, Staffordshire is open occasionally for special events (as advertised locally).

WELD OF CHIDEOCK

Mr Charles Weld.

DIVERSIFICATION is the key to the survival of many family seats. Nowhere is this exemplified more encouragingly than on the flourishing estate of Chideock in Dorset, home of the highly successful controlled-circulation magazine publisher Charles Weld, who recently let the manor house to the Duke and Duchess of York for a spell while the Duke was stationed at Portland.

The Welds, a branch of one of the great Catholic families of England, have owned the Chideock estate between Bridport and Lyme Regis since the beginning of the 19th century. Before the Second World War, however, its future as a family seat seemed bleak. The house was let out and at a time of agricultural slump the land was unprofitable.

During the war Chideock housed evacuees, a school and was then used as a sugar depot. In 1956 Lieutenant-Colonel Humphrey Weld, Charles's father, retired from the Army after a distinguished career in which he won the Military Cross in Tunisia, commanded his regiment, the Queen's Bays, and ended up as military attaché in Washington. Colonel Weld, who is a Deputy Lieutenant for Dorest and was formerly chairman of the Bridport bench, removed the Victorian wing of the house and worked hard to resuscitate the Chideock estate. It thus affords him particular satisfaction that the metropolitan enterprise of his son and heir has now enabled the place to flourish.

Having made the estate over to his son in 1971, the Colonel and his wife, Fanny (a cousin of Lord Lovat's), moved into a pleasing orangery of his own design nearby in 1984. Charles Weld now runs the 1,000-acre estate with the help of an able management team led by his cousin Michael Rous (a member of the family headed by the exuberant Australian Earl of Stradbroke).

All the land is in hand, some 850 acres being farmed (corn and grass) in partnership by a farm manager, Ian Freeland. More than 1,400 breeding ewes and 280 ewe lambs are housed in an enormous sheep shed up on the hill near the coastal road where the estate is due to open a new farm shop with a play area for children.

Thirteen people are currently employed on the Chideock estate. Four of these work in the woods under Dickon Hawker, whose company Dorset Woodlands also services three other estates in the neighbourhood. The 150 acres of woods at Chideock are managed according to a broadleaved policy so as to supply plenty of game cover. A major planting programme is currently in operation: some 3,500 trees went in last year and Mr Hawker reckons that this year's total should reach 6,000.

During my visit to Chideock a breezily enjoyable shooting party was in full swing despite the bitterly cold weather. There is a syndicate of three Guns and six half-Guns. The estate is shot for ten days a year, with two let days. About 3,000 pheasants and 600 partridges (unkown at Chideock a generation ago) are put down and half-a-dozen flight ponds have been installed for duck.

Chideock has a fine sporting tradition. The Seavington Hunt, of which Colonel

Opposite
Chideock Manor, Dorset: view across lake.

Chideock Manor: chapel.

chimneypieces from old Chideock Castle which was slighted by the Cromwellians in 1645 after a series of vicissitudes in the Civil War during which the castle was a royalist stronghold.

The name of Chideock is Ancient British in origin and means 'the wooded place'. In the *Domesday Book* 'Cidihoc' was part of an extensive royal estate. By the early 13th century the manor had become vested in the Mandeville family and in 1248 Geoffrey de Mandeville granted it for life to Thomas le Bretthun (whose daughter married the ancestor of the de Chideockes) on condition that he built a timber hall there.

In 1450 the last Sir John de Chideocke died leaving two daughters, one of whom married Sir John Arundell of Lanherne, Cornwall, in which famous Catholic family the manor remained until 1802. In that year the 8th Lord Arundell of Wardour, whose mother was the heiress of the Cornish Arundells, sold Chideock to his cousin Thomas Weld.

Thomas Weld had already inherited several estates from his childless brother Edward (first husband of the famous Mrs Fitzherbert) including Lulworth in Dorset and Stonyhurst and Leagram in Lancashire. The Welds descend from William de Welde, Sheriff of London in 1352. They moved to Dorset in the 17th century, acquiring large estates from the Howard family.

Thomas's portrait at Chideock shows him in a trooper's uniform of the Rangers Volunteer Yeomanry as Roman Catholics were not then allowed to hold commissions in the Army. A staunch upholder of the old faith, Thomas had been educated at the English Academy at Liege. When this establishment was expelled by the armies of Revolutionary France in 1794, Weld offered Stonyhurst as a substitute and so it became a Catholic public school and the principal home of the English Jesuits.

Lulworth passed to Thomas's eldest son and namesake who became Cardinal Weld (the first Englishman to have a seat in the conclave since the pontificate of Clement IX) and made over the estate to his brother Joseph, ancestor of the present senior line of the Welds. Leagram went to Thomas's eighth son whereas Chideock was inherited on Thomas's death in 1810 by his sixth son, Humphrey Weld.

At the time Humphrey Weld inherited the Chideock estate there was a fairly modest farmhouse on the site of the present house with a barn attached. In an

Weld acted as Master in the late 1950s, meets on the estate and there is trout fishing on the recently relandscaped lake. On the new ornamental duck pond next door, Colonel Weld proudly points out exotic imports from Slimbridge including white-fronted geese, mandarin duck, red-crested pochard and Chiloe widgeon.

The Colonel, who used to ride in point-to-points, and his son share a love of the Turf and owned the useful hurdler Autumn Song a few seasons back. Charles Weld has recently restored the stables near the house and plans to acquire some brood mares.

Among the notable recent restoration work at Chideock has been the wholesale renovation of the handsomely arcaded Carters Lane Barn of 1841. The main house itself has been reroofed, its conservatory rebuilt and the back kitchen rearranged.

The back kitchen and the dining-room contain two magnificent emblematic

upper room of this barn Mass had continued to be said since the destruction of the old castle. Between 1810 and 1815 Humphrey Weld built the present bow-fronted house of attractive yellowish stone from the local quarry, as well as a chapel attached on the site of the old barn.

Humphrey's son Charles, who inherited Chideock in 1852, felt the chapel, in particular, was somewhat inadequate. A talented artist and architect, Charles proceeded to rebuild the chapel to his own gorgeously elaborate Romanesque design. The fine paintings on the altar, the wall and roof decorations in general and the sculptures of the capitals in the impressive shafts were all the personal work of Charles Weld. The new church of Our Lady, Queen of Martyrs, and St Ignatius was completed in 1874 and opened by Bishop Vaughan, cousin of this great Catholic dynasty.

Today the chapel is used regularly for worship and attached to it is the Chideock Museum, which presents an absorbing view of the social history of the village and the estate.

The cash for Charles's improvements to the chapel, house and estate would appear to have come from his wife, Mary Davison-Bland, the daughter of a Yorkshire coal baron. Charles was a barrister, JP, traveller and collector.

It was in his time that the extraordinary 'Jawbones Gate' was erected on the estate, formed from the remains of a whale washed up on the beach. In those days the Chideock estate went right down to the sea but in recent years the outlying coastal property has been vested in the National Trust's Enterprise Neptune.

Upon Charles's death in 1885 Chideock passed to his younger brother Sir Frederick Weld, who had been prime minister of New Zealand during the Maori War, served as governor of Western Australia, Tasmania and the Straits Settlements and established a British agency in Pahang. Both Port Weld, Perak, and the exclusive Weld Club in Perth are named after this eminent Victorian empire-builder.

Following Sir Frederick's death in 1891, his widow, the former Filumena March-Phillipps de Lisle, became a Benedictine nun at Kiloumein Abbey, Fort Augustus, where her daughter Edith was to become the first Abbess in Scotland since the Reformation. Chideock was inherited by Sir Frederick's eldest son, Humphrey, who served his country as a soldier in the yeomanry, JP, county councillor and High Sheriff.

Colonel Weld, their son, points out that in 1991, if he is spared, there will have been only two generations across a century at Chideock. With the enthusiasm and energy of his son Charles, formerly a jackaroo and a lieutenant in the Coldstream Guards, being applied to this rejuvenated estate, one can be equally confident about the 21st century.

The Chideock Museum, attached to the Catholic church by the manor, is open to the public and various events are held (as advertised) on the estate.

Left
Chideock: as it was *c* 1915, before removal of Victorian accretions.

Below
Chideock: dining-room chimneypiece removed from Chideock Castle.

DUCKWORTH OF ORCHARDLEIGH

Orchardleigh Park, Somerset: view across lake to garden front.

A FRENCH château is an improbable sight to come across in the middle of rolling West Country parkland but, thanks to the skill of its architect, Thomas Henry Wyatt, Orchardleigh Park near Frome in Somerset succeeds as a splendid example of spiky Victorian architecture.

When William Duckworth, of a Lancastrian legal family that had made its fortune in Manchester property, bought the Orchardleigh estate in 1855 he favoured a neo-Elizabethan design for the new house to be built on a plateau above the luxuriant lakes in the valley. Wyatt, a member of the celebrated architectural dynasty of that name and a prolific designer of churches and lunatic asylums, as well as of country houses, persuaded his client to vary the skyline with a touch of the French Renaissance.

The tower, the doubtful Duckworth was assured by Wyatt, was 'quite in keeping with foreign châteaux'. The new squire's son, the Reverend W. A. Duckworth, found 'the saddleback roof tower decidedly objectionable at first, tho' the impression may wear off when we live there'. In any event, Orchardleigh remained the seat of the Duckworth family and is now the home of the octogenarian Arthur Duckworth, the former MP for Shrewsbury, Somerset county councillor

Opposite
Orchardleigh: hall and staircase.

and magistrate, and of his third wife, Frances.

The Duckworths acquired the property from the receiver in bankruptcy of the colourful Sir Thomas Mostyn-Champneys, 2nd (and last) Baronet, who had spent some £100,000 (seven million pounds in today's money) on embellishing the estate with lakes, lodges and other extravagances. 'His love of show was his undoing,' commented *The Somerset Standard* sagely. As High Sheriff of the county in 1800 the profligate squire found it necessary to employ two dozen 'javelin men, suitably dressed in imposing costumes and quite a retinue of attendants' to help him carry out his ceremonial duties.

When the Duke of Gloucester paid him a visit, Champneys built a lodge and a large banqueting room in HRH's honour. The jollifications included one dinner which began bizarrely with the guests discovering a variety of live birds and small animals under the covers on their plates. On his return to Orchardleigh from his second spell in the King's Bench prison for debt, Sir Thomas could not resist one more triumphant show—the tenantry were splendidly fitted up in white costumes and ribbons for a lavish programme of entertainment.

Sir Thomas was the fourth Champneys to serve as Sheriff of Somerset. The family had been seated at Orchardleigh from before 1440 according to the distinguished antiquary and local historian Michael McGarvie of Frome, whose publications include *Orchardleigh House* (an account of its building based on the diaries of the Reverend W. A. Duckworth) and *Sir Henry Newbolt and Orchardleigh*.

In his novel *The Old Country* (1906) Newbolt, who was married to Mr Duckworth's daughter, Margaret, and whose ashes are buried at Orchardleigh, portrays the place as Gardenleigh: 'Beneath them lay the lakes and the church on its island, and far away, from the opposite side of the valley, Gardenleigh looked across at them, its gray stone gables and mullions all yellow in the light of the westering sun.'

The other literary connection of the family is that Mr Duckworth's nephew, Gerald Duckworth, who founded the publishing house of that name, was a stepbrother of Virginia Woolf.

Newbolt's novel *The Old Country* also features a considerably less flattering portrait of the Champneys's old manor house: 'a patchwork of inconveniences, with its narrow 14th-century (*sic*) yard, low

Mr and Mrs Arthur Duckworth.

Orchardleigh Park, near Frome, Somerset, is open by appointment to groups.

1856 to 1858. Wyatt's design was executed by D. Jones of Bradford-on-Avon, with joinery by Holland of London and ironwork by Cockey of Frome. Of Bradford stone, with Bath stone dressings, the building materials were fire-proof wrought-iron girders and concrete.

The interior has an agreeably spacious plan. There is fine maplewood and satinwood decoration, particularly in the library; a bas relief in the dining-room ceiling; an ornate frieze and marble columns in the drawing-room; and a grandoise wooden staircase. It is 19th-century craftsmanship of a high order.

The impressive terraces on the garden front, and a lower geometrical flower garden, were laid out by a Mr Page, a mid-19th-century landscaper. The 'island church' was restored by Mr Duckworth, who succeeded his father at Orchardleigh in 1876, to the designs of Sir Giles Gilbert Scott.

The discovery of a canine skeleton (supposedly that of a mastiff which saved the life of the first Champneys baronet) during the restoration of the church inspired Sir Henry Newbolt's ballad *Fidele's Grassy Tomb*; though, as Mr McGarvie points out, Sir Thomas's dog was actually a Prussian poodle and is buried under a monument at Wood Lodge, a rustic cottage in the extensive park.

Today the Orchardleigh estate runs to some 2,000 acres with a home farm (dairy and beef) of 500 acres and 300 acres of lovely oak woods. There is a private shooting syndicate, coarse fishing in the 24 acres of lakes and the South and West Wiltshire Hunt sometimes meets here. The present owner, Arthur Duckworth, has stylishly restored the house since its spoilation by the military in the Second World War; the ten-year overhaul that ensued after derequisition was complete in all respects save for the replacements of the glass in Wyatt's ambitious conservatory.

Mr Duckworth has five daughters (three by his first marriage, two by his second). As well as being a politician, public servant and farmer, he has been a discerning patron of the arts. His portrait in the drawing-room was painted by Anthony Devas and there is an engaging description of the squire of Orchardleigh in Nicolette Devas's Bohemian memoirs, *Two Flamboyant Fathers*: 'He could move with ease from a shoot lunch on his estate in Somerset to our kitchen table [in Chelsea]; a patron without patronage'

Tudor kitchens and great Queen Anne front out of all proportion. Low-lying, too, and damp, no doubt, close by the water from which the frogs were traditionally reported to have come at times in troops to serenade the drawing-room window'. The Duckworths pulled down the old house in 1860; its appearance is recorded in drawings and early photographs at the National Monuments Record.

The NMR also has copies of the remarkable series of photographs taken during the construction of the new house from

PART IV

THE 20th CENTURY

FOSTER OF LEXHAM

Mr and Mrs William Foster with
their eldest son, Neil.

A VISITOR to Lexham Hall in Norfolk, seeing a Dutch gable on the south front of the house, observed 'William and Mary, I suppose?' 'No', replied the owner of this remarkable family seat, William Foster, 'William and Jean'.

Many other features of East Lexham, apart from the Hall itself—the gardens, the bridges, the vernacular farm buildings, the roads, the model estate village with its charming ornamental 'butter market' and pond, the good order of the Saxon church—also owe almost everything to the foresight and vision of Mr Foster and his wife Jean (*née* Urquhart).

In 1946 they courageously bought a virtually derelict property. 'The place looked a wreck,' Mr Foster recalls. 'It was in such a deplorable state that when I look at the pictures of the place as it was in 1946 I feel quite sick.' The Hall (many of is windows shattered by an exploding bomber) and the park had been used as a military dump. The houses in the village were in equally bad condition.

'I often wonder why we decided to try to buy Lexham,' says Mr Foster, who is a member of the great Yorkshire wool dynasty of John Foster and Son of Bradford.

Lexham Hall, Norfolk: staircase.

'Probably it was because we felt it had the foundations for a good place. Moreover, the land looked right and as we were young we felt that with a little bit of luck we might be able to make a good job of it. Not even the Nissen huts on the park deterred us.'

Originally there was a manor house called Rouse's on a moated site south-west of the present Lexham Hall. Rouse's was abandoned in the later Middle Ages; the Wrights of Weeting, who acquired the manor in 1568, lived in a new house on or about the present site. In the 1630s John Wright rebuilt this house to form the core of the present-day Hall.

Wright later sold the property to a Richard Moore whose executors conveyed it in 1673 to Sir Philip Wodehouse, 3rd Baronet, MP, of Kimberley, 'a man of great learning and a skilled musician'. Sir Philip's grandfather and namesake, the 1st Baronet, had acquired East Lexham Manor (not to be confused with Rouse's) almost a century earlier.

Lexham Hall remained in the owner-

Lexham Hall: east (entrance) front.

ship of the Wodehouses until the beginning of the 19th century. Significant remodellings were carried out in the early years of the 18th century by Edmund Wodehouse and in the 1770s by John Wodehouse, son and heir of Sir Armine Wodehouse, 5th Baronet. The immortal humorist P. G. Wodehouse descends from John's younger brother.

There exists a design for John Wodehouse's study at Lexham by the Palladian architect John Sanderson, dated 1770. Although there is no further evidence that Sanderson was responsible for any other work at Lexham he is known to have worked at the Wodehouses' principal seat of Kimberley at about this time. 'Capability' Brown had landscaped the park at Kimberley a few years before and this clearly influenced Wodehouse's operations in the park at Lexham in 1776.

The following year, 1777, John succeeded to the baronetcy and to Kimberley, later being created a peer. Lexham was evantually sold to the tenant, John Hyde, who in turn sold out to Frederick Keppel, son of the Dean of Windsor.

The Keppels made various additions to the Hall and great improvements to the cottages, barns and other farm buildings. They continued to own Lexham until shortly before the First World War. Two World Wars and adverse economic conditions caused a slow but steady deterioration until the renaissance brought about by 'William and Jean'.

Lexham: library.

To restore the Hall the Fosters called in the distinguished Norwich architect James Fletcher-Watson, a disciple of Sir Edwin Lutyens. 'When he arrived,' Mr Foster recalls, 'he looked and said "Your'e going to have a marvellous house!" It was the first bit of good cheer we had had since buying the place.'

Between 1947 and 1949 Fletcher-Watson removed the Victorian accretions to produce a stylish and handsome four-square house. Forty years on, it is by no means easy to tell which is 18th-century and which is 20th-century work.

The north front is, in fact, the earliest of the facades, though the old entrance door became a window in Fletcher-Watson's remodelling. The central porch on the east front and the bow, doorway and Dutch gable on the south front are all Fletcher-Watson. He was also largely responsible for the interior, the Fosters

Lexham: drawing-room.

having brought in some fine fireplaces.

The panelled library is a particularly satisfying Fletcher-Watson creation. The dining-room has a classical chimneypiece and attractive recesses; the drawing-room a pretty frieze, a carving supposedly by Grinling Gibbons and a portrait of Mr Foster as High Sheriff of Norfolk in 1969.

Mr Foster, born in 1911, was educated at Wellington and Corpus Christi, Oxford. He was called to the Bar before the Second World War, in which he served with the Black Watch, and has pursued business interests in metals and mining, as well as continuing the family's connection with the Black Dyke Mills in Yorkshire.

Today the flourishing 3,800-acre estate is run in partnership with his eldest son, Neil, who lives in the partly Elizabethan Church Farm. The various enterprises include a 2,150-acre home farm—arable, plus a 350-sow breeding unit; 380 acres of woodland and a forestry department selling 10,000 stakes a year; and the award-winning Lexham Hall Vineyard which annually produces 14,000 bottles of dry, white, mild and fruity wine. With the help of the Council for Small Industries in Rural Areas, the estate has converted some of the old farm buildings into workshops for crafts and high-technology.

The 60-acre Litcham Common on the estate, noted for its heathland, wood and scrub, has recently been declared a Local Nature Reserve. The Hall gardens, which boast an original 'crinkle-crankle wall' are open occasionally for charity.

Mr Foster is an honorary vice-president of the British Field Sports Society and encourages sport at Lexham, which is near the centre of the West Norfolk Foxhounds and Norfolk Beagles and is in some of the best shooting country in West Norfolk.

Mr and Mrs Foster's second son is Richard Foster the artist, who has captured Lexham's special atmosphere in some of his paintings. It has an uncanny feeling of, in Tennyson's words, 'all things in order stored'—as if it has always been like this, the *beau ideal* of a country estate.

> *Lexham Hall, Litcham, near Kings Lynn, Norfolk, is not open to the public, though the gardens are open occasionally as advertised.*

Lexham: hallway.

Lexham: south front as it was in 1947.

PINNEY OF BETTISCOMBE

The Pinneys seem to have first come to Bettiscombe as bailiffs for the lord of the manor in the 16th century after it had ceased to be ecclesiastical land at the Reformation. Although they did not own the freehold, they stayed on, living in the manor house and holding part of the property on a 'lease of lives' from the Browns of Frampton.

In the 17th century Bettiscombe was the home of John Pinney, the Puritan divine and lace manufacturer. He had a short-lived licence of 1672 from Charles II to hold Presbyterian meetings in the house, having earlier been ejected as Vicar of Broadwindsor. Of John Pinney's sons, the youngest, Azariah, fought for Monmouth at Sedgemoor in 1685 and was condemned to slavery at Dorchester Assizes by the notorious Judge Jeffreys. However, his sister, Hester, managed to 'buy' him for approximately the price of a pound of thread and he went as a banished but free man to the West Indies where he became a sugar planter.

The divine's eldest son, Nathaniel Pinney, who married Naomi Gay (a cousin or perhaps an aunt of the author of *The Beggar's Opera*), rebuilt the existing house at Bettiscombe in 1694.

Further improvements, including the staircase, a perfectly-proportioned grand staircase-in-miniature, were made in the early 18th century. There have been few changes since then, except for the pedi-

Bettiscombe: rear elevation.

MICHAEL PINNEY has never forgotten his first sight of Bettiscombe Manor, near Bridport. As a boy, walking down the hill from his family's Georgian mansion, the nearby Racedown, he fell instantly in love with Bettiscombe, whose exquisite ensemble of manor house, outbuildings and landscape might be straight from the pages of Thomas Hardy.

This unspoilt and unpretentious small Dorset manor house with family associations going back to Tudor times had been given up in the 19th century because it was no longer grand enough for the prosperous Pinneys. He determined that one day he would return to live there.

At this time Bettiscombe belonged to the Young family but later, by a lucky chance, Mr Pinney learnt that they would be prepared to sell the freehold of the 500-acre estate to him as they had 'always wanted a Pinney to have it'. Thus, in 1934, he and his bride, Betty Cooke, the artist, poster and textile designer and novelist, were able to make their home there.

Right
Bettiscombe Manor, Dorset: staircase.

Bettiscombe Manor: entrance front.

mented hood with Doric entablature over the present front door, which seems to have been added in about 1800. The north (garden) door, with a shell hood resting on scrolled brackets, dates from the 1694 remodelling.

Built of attractive red brick made in a kiln on the site, Bettiscombe is basically a small Tudor house, probably of much older foundations, that has been enlarged. The stone dressings are of Ham Hill stone. Inside there is pleasantly restrained panelling of impressive quality throughout.

The hall is the outstanding interior with its triple-arched screen, flagstone floor and early (1748) Reynolds of Nathaniel Pinney's grandson, another Azariah Pin-

ney, who was High Sheriff of Dorset in 1749. The beams in the hall, which have similar oakleaf motifs to those found at Forde Abbey not far away, date from 1540. Other notable features include the overmantel in the morning room; a clock of 1691 by one Richard Pinney of Beaminister; and the agreeably untouched walk-in cupboards in the bedrooms. The atmosphere, both inside and out, has a timeless quality.

Upon the High Sheriff's death in 1760, Bettiscombe passed to his cousin, John Frederick Pinney (the rebel Azariah's grandson), who was MP for Bridport and built Racedown at the end of Pilsdon Hill. Following the MP's death from gout shortly afterwards the family estates were

Bettiscombe: hall.

divided and Bettiscombe was inherited by another cousin, John Pretor (later Pretor-Pinney). As described in the economic history *A West India Fortune*, John Pretor-Pinney became a Caribbean tycoon. He ceased to live at Bettiscombe, basing himself at a handsome town house in Bristol (now known as the Georgian House and open as a museum of the period), where Coleridge was to meet Wordsworth for the first time in 1795. The Pinneys later lent Racedown to Wordsworth and his sister, Dorothy.

The Bettiscombe days seemed forgotten as the family went up in the world. John Pretor-Pinney's son and namesake was a rich Radical who divided his time between a corner house in Berkeley Square and his country estate in Somerton Erleigh in Somerset. However, his spinster daughter, Anna Maria, became interested in Bettiscombe after delving in the copious family papers (now housed in the library of Bristol University) and visited the old house in 1847. The legend that the famous 'Screaming Skull' of Bettiscombe (which she saw in the house) was that of a negro slave from the Pinneys' West Indian plantations who had laid a curse on his master, came about following Anna Maria's visit.

This Victorian myth and other numerous pieces of folklore are firmly dealt with in Michael Pinney's own lucid account of the *Legends and History of Bettiscombe*. By scientific pronouncement the Screaming Skull (probably discovered at the time of the rebuilding of 1694) is the fossilised cranium of a young white woman that has been buried for at least 1,500 years. 'It is the luck, not the curse of Bettiscombe, going back to very ancient sacrifice,' says Mr Pinney, who is a poet and has published books under the imprint of the

Bettiscombe Press.

Since returning to Bettiscombe more than 50 years ago, the present Pinney Lord of the Manor has carried out much sensitive restoration work (recently with the help of grants) and is currently tackling an outbreak of dry rot in the hall. His late wife, Betty, picked out the panelling in charmingly muted colours, and the house is adorned with her pictures and fabrics. Some of this work, together with her well-known posters of the 1930s and 1940s, which used to cheer up journeys on the old Southern Railway, was recently shown in a special exhibition at the Dorchester Museum.

The Pinney's elder son Azariah's epic march of a flock of sheep from Scotland to Exmoor was the subject of a memorable television documentary. The younger son, Charlie, who breeds carthorses, is married to the journalist Lucy Dilke, sister-in-law of the ill-fated Georgi Markov, who was murdered with a poisoned umbrella ferrule in London in 1978.

Mr Pinney has sold two of the farms on the estate to their tenants and has opened negotiations with the Dorset Naturalist Trust to make the land near the house into a nature reserve. A keen archaeologist, Mr Pinney remains the tenant of the historic monument on the estate, the excavation site known as Pilsdon Pen which is now owned by the National Trust.

'Bettiscombe', Mr Pinney says, 'is not a place of a curse at all, but in spite of the ancient sacrifice, in spite of the owning of slaves, a house of kindliness and peace.'

Above
Bettiscombe: bedroom with walk-in cupboard.

Left
Mr Michael Pinney.

Bettiscombe Manor, near Bridport, Dorset, is open to the public by appointment.

ROPNER OF THORP PERROW

Thorp Perrow, Yorkshire: entrance front across lake.

Opposite
Thorpe Perrow: ballroom.

I N THE middle of the last century an enterprising immigrant named Robert Ropner arrived, virtually penniless, in the north-east of England from Germany. Despite this difficult beginning he managed to establish a fleet of steamships in West Hartlepool, as well as a shipbuilding company in Stockton-on-Tees. He became the squire of Preston Hall, a noted citizen of Co Durham, MP for Stockton, a knight and a baronet, and founded an industrial dynasty.

In 1927, three years after Sir Robert's death, his third son, William, bought the estate of Thorp Perrow, near Snape in the old North Riding of Yorkshire, now the seat of his grandson, Sir John Ropner, 2nd Baronet, Joint-Master of the Bedale.

Thorp Perrow's history goes back much further than the exterior of the handsome house—ostensibly late-Georgian with Edwardian embellishments—might suggest. The name of the property derives from the 13th-century marriage between the Thorp heiress and William de Pirrowe from Norfolk. When it passed from the hands of their descend-ants in the middle of the 15th century, it was bought by the eminent lawyer, Sir Robert Danby, Chief Justice of the Court of Common Pleas, who is said to have been killed (and not accidentally) by his gamekeeper.

The Danbys of Thorp Perrow extended their landholdings by judicious alliances, acquiring the historic Snape Castle, still part of the estate, through the marriage of Sir Christopher Danby to a sister of John Nevill, 3rd Lord Latimer—the first husband of Henry VIII's sixth wife, Catherine Parr.

There is a clue to how the old manor house looked in an early-18th-century drawing by Samuel Buck. Although this shows a contemporary façade of nine bays, with a fine new doorway, the battlemented towers look much earlier, indicating that the Tudor Thorp Perrow may have been quadrangular with corner towers enclosing a central courtyard.

Buck was recording the alterations made by John Milbank, who bought the estate at the end of the 17th century. The Milbanks, a branch of the Newcastle merchant adventuring family that later produced Byron's wife, remained the squires of Thorp Perrow for almost exactly 200 years. Halfway through their tenure, in about 1800, John Milbank's great-grandson, William, transformed the house with the help of the architect John Foss of Richmond in the North Riding.

The house was 'new modelled and in great part rebuilt', its façade being of 11 bays, with a three-bay pediment and what Pevsner describes as 'beautifully detailed' Venetian windows at either end with Adamesque super-arches. The internal decoration, notably the ceiling of the magnificent 500-foot long ballroom, was in the manner of James Wyatt, who was clearly a strong influence on Foss.

The Milbanks, who later became baronets, eventually settled on their other estate, Barningham near Richmond (*see* PART II) and sold Thorp Perrow in 1898 to Herbert Allfrey, of a Berkshire land-owning family, who called in the fashionable York architect Thomas Brierley to

Above
Thorpe Perrow: principal bedroom.

Opposite
Thorp Perrow: arboretum.

Above
Sir John and Lady Ropner, with Carolyn, Henry and Annabel.

Thorp Perrow, near Snape, North Yorkshire, is not open to the public (though private visits for groups can be arranged by appointment).

modernise the property. Brierley added the *porte-cochère*, redecorated much of the interior in the Edwardian Classical mode and built the rather sober stables, with 21 boxes.

But, despite having set himself up in some style at Thorp Perrow, Allfrey did not stay long. In 1904 the estate was bought by the West Hartlepool ship-builder, Sir William Gray, 1st Baronet, who proceeded to install the three features considered indispensable to the Edwardian magnate: a billiards room, an organ in its own panelled hall and a splendid indoor swimming-pool, with changing rooms.

The Grays and the Ropners were friendly rivals in the same business. In 1921 Sir William Gray's youngest daughter married William Ropner's second son and six years later William Ropner bought Thorp Perrow from the Grays, with a view to it becoming the seat of his eldest son, Leonard.

Leonard Ropner went into the family shipping business and was a Member of Parliament for 40 years, being created a baronet in 1952. Essentially an outdoor man, his passions were big-game hunting, racing motor-cars and, above all, trees. His great achievement at Thorp Perrow

was the world-famous arboretum he created from 1936 onwards on some 60 acres of open parkland given to him by his father.

When he died in 1977 Sir Leonard had planted 2,049 different species. Some were too tender to withstand Yorkshire conditions, some were unsuited to the soil, and others have lived out their alloted span; but more than 1,500 have survived and flourish. Several are the largest of their kind and some are the only specimens at present recorded in Britain. The Temple built to Sir Leonard's memory at Thorp Perrow bears the inscription (borrowed from that to Sir Christopher Wren): 'For his memorial look around you'.

'To inherit Thorp Perrow was a privilege,' says Sir Leonard's son and successor, Sir John Ropner, 2nd Baronet, 'but with privilege comes responsibility. As I intended to leave the estate in a better financial state than when I inherited, this has meant adapting to modern-day conditions and squeezing revenue from sources only recently considered.' Just as Sir John and his cousins in the Ropner family business have diversified from shipping into insurance, engineering and property, so has the commercial potential of Thorp Perrow been developed.

In 1977 Sir John needed to find about half a million pounds to keep Thorp Perrow solvent. Some 300 acres of the estate were sold, leaving about 2,500 acres. After an uneconomic spell running the home farm (arable, dairy and sheep), Sir John made over the 800 acres formerly 'in hand' to a company called Snape Castle Farms Limited for a period of 20 years.

The arboretum catalogued by John Beach, is now open to the public on a regular basis from the end of March to the end of October; the Thorp Perrow Nurseries on the estate help to cover the cost of the three gardeners by selling trees and shrubs. As well as tending the 350 acres of woodland, two foresters earn their keep by making agricultural fencing for commercial sale and one doubles as a gamekeeper.

Having discovered that the terrain of Thorp Perrow is not conducive to high birds, Sir John has scaled down his initial plans to run a commercial shoot on the estate. 'However,' he says, 'we put down about a thousand pheasants a year and it makes an agreeable small family shoot, particularly for those, so to speak, on the nursery slopes.' The fishing on the two lakes is let.

'To keep the roof on the house,' Sir John says, 'we have been entertaining paying guests at Thorp Perrow. He and his second wife, the former Auriol Mackeson-Sandbach, give lavish house parties for separate groups of shooters and art enthusiasts, drawn mainly from America and the Continent.

Some of the house parties are now being marketed through Abercrombie and Kent, the travel agents. Colonel Kit Egerton of Sporting Services arranges top quality sport for the shooters on nearby estates, while 'Art Experience' (an enterprise of Malise Ropner, former wife of one of Sir John's cousins), looks after the cultural side.

As well as supervising the catering Auriol Ropner is a knowledgeable guide to the decoration and contents of Thorp Perrow. She was responsible for the Georgian restoration of the previously 'Edwardianised' library; the chimney-piece, with a head presumed to be that of Lord Rockingham, was rescued from the gun room in a dilapidated condition. Many of the contents, including the Radcliffe family portraits, were originally from Hitchin Priory, former seat of Sir John Ropner's first wife, Milet Delmé-Radcliffe.

FORBES ADAM OF SKIPWITH

Skipwith Hall, Yorkshire: old entrance hall.

I T IS an aristocratic axiom that one needs a substantial estate to support a large country house. When the land goes, the house soon follows. Conversely, however, when the big house goes, it does not necessarily mean the end of the family's connection with the estate.

Some landowners, faced with echoing piles devasted by the exigencies of wartime and capital taxation, have opted for a more convenient new residence nearby. Others, such as the Forbes Adam family in the old East Riding of Yorkshire, have sensibly repaired to a comparatively modest manor house already standing elsewhere on their ancestral acres.

Thus, though the principal seat of Escrick Park—familiar to country-house cricketers as the home ground of the Yorkshire Gentlemen—was sold by the Forbes Adams in 1972, the family holdings hereabouts still run to some 7,000 acres. Mr Nigel Forbes Adam is seated a few miles down the road from Escrick at the comfortable, red-brick Skipwith Hall.

The village of Skipwith appears in *Domesday Book* as 'Schipewic' and the manor was long held by the de Stutevilles

Opposite
Skipwith Hall: south front.

Skipwith: dining-room.

appear that the diarist had some sort of connection with the owners of these seats, the Parker family. Certainly the Parkers intermarried with the Toulsons of Skipwith in the 18th century.

In the early 19th century a younger son of the Alkincoats line, John Parker, took the surname of Toulson on becoming the squire of Skipwith. His descendants included the two Lords Parker of Waddington (one a Lord of Appeal in Ordinary, the other Lord Chief Justice), another High Court Judge (in Madras) and Dame Ellen Pinsent, who distinguished herself on the Royal Commission on 'the Care and Control of the Feeble-Minded'. The last of the family to live at Skipwith was Miss Mary Parker, John Parker-Toulson's granddaughter.

The 1780 diary also contains a reference to 'Mr Thompson's House and Stables—most elegant & just finished ...' This is Escrick Park which had been bought from the Howards a century earlier by Sir Henry Thompson, a prosperous wine merchant and sometime Lord Mayor of York. 'Mr Thompson' was the dilettante Whig MP, Beilby Thompson, who was 'not fond of doing for above a fortnight a year'. The new house and stables at Escrick were the work of Carr of York.

In the 19th century the Escrick estate was inherited by Beilby Thompson's grandson, Sir Paul Lawley-Thompson, 8th Baronet (brother-in-law of Lady Conyngham, one of the massive marchionesses who accommodated George IV), created Baron Wenlock in 1839. The 3rd Lord Wenlock added the neighbouring Skipwith estate to his holdings of more than 20,000 acres in the early years of this century when he also added the east wing to Skipwith Hall (which contains the agreeably panelled library).

Upon the death of the 3rd Baron in 1912 (*The Times* obituary noted 'his devotion to sport, and skill in many of its forms'), the Escrick estate passed to his only child, the Honourable Irene Lawley. In 1920 she married Colin Forbes Adam, a younger son of Sir Frank Forbes Adam, 1st Baronet, sometimes president of the Bank of Bombay, and himself a member of the Indian Civil Service.

For ten years the Forbes Adams lived in the big house at Escrick. Then in 1930 they decided to make their home at Skipwith where they added the west wing (which contains the sunny drawing-room) and switched the entrance from the south front to the north. Escrick eventually became a girls' school.

(who later took the name of Skipwith). There seems to have been an early 17th century farmhouse on the site of the present Skipwith Hall. This was aggrandised in about 1698 into the seven-bay structure we see at the centre of the house today (the east and west wings were added in 1904 and 1930 respectively). The hall retains its original flagstones.

Skipwith was formerly the seat of the Toulson family but a diverting description, in an unpublished diary among the muniments, of a visit to the Hall in 1780, mentions a family called Walton as living there. The anonymous diarist (clearly female) arrived at Skipwith during a heatwave on 25 July:

> Mr & Mrs Walton received me with the greatest civility—she shewed me all over her good House which is convenient—& as perfectly clean, exact and nice as Mr Lascelles's [Harewood, no less] ... Mr Walton took me into all his stables, barns, coach-house, & outbuildings, into all the gardens, stores, hot houses & hot walls, which are most large and handsome & well stocked with all kinds of good fruits—we never sat down ...

The Waltons seemed to enjoy the pleasures of the table—'the usual salmon just got out of the river' and 'a fine haunch of venison ... it was well done'—though our observer did not care for 'all sorts of flying, biting animals in the house'.

Judging from the references to Browsholme and Alkincoats in the diary it would

The present squire, Nigel Forbes Adam, a JP, chairman of the National Trust's Yorkshire regional committee and former High Sheriff, is the youngest son of Colin and Irene. Of their other children, Timothy married the actress Penelope Munday and went into the Church; Desmond married the only daughter of Sir Oswald Mosley and was killed in an accident in 1958; and Virginia married that underrated novelist, the late Hugo Charteris.

Nigel also married an actress, Teresa Moor, the sister of his old Cambridge friend, the theatre director Toby Robertson. One of the outbuildings at Skipwith houses a small theatre created by Irene. Nigel and Teresa's second son, Titus, has also gone on the stage. Of the others, Charles is in the city, Pip is a pilot and Harry is a gamekeeper on the family estate.

Nigel farms some 1,700 acres in hand—all arable. The estate includes Skipwith Common, a remarkable 800-acre Site of Special Scientific Interest noted for its primeval variety of vegetation, plants, insects and bird species. Part of the Common is leased to the Yorkshire Wildlife Trust which arranges access.

The Skipwith gardens are also open occasionally to the public. The features include statuary, a dovecote designed by Teresa and a mulberry tree contemporary with the house.

When Nigel and Teresa Forbes Adam moved into Skipwith 20 years ago, they carried out a thorough renovation and restoration with the help of the prolific country house architect, Sir Martyn Beckett, Bt. The result is a series of exceptionally sympathetic interiors. Delicately painted panelling, pilasters, alcoves and other satisfying architectural features constantly please the eye. The 18th-century pine staircase has an unusually ornate ceiling for such a delightfully unpretentious manor house.

Skipwith: staircase.

Skipwith Hall, near Selby, Yorkshire, is not open to the pubic, though the gardens are open occasionally as advertised.

BROOKS OF PEOVER

Mr Randle Brooks and his son, Henry, in the dining-room of Peover Hall, Cheshire.

THE delightful Elizabethan manor house at Over Peover in Cheshire, Peover Hall, was begun in 1585 by Sir Randle Mainwaring; the date is inscribed over the doorway at the side of the entrance block. The Mainwarings remained at Peover (pronounced '*Peever*') until earlier this century and the house has recently been sympathetically restored by the Brooks family.

The Mainwarings had been seated at Over Peover for several centuries before Sir Randle built the Elizabethan house. The previous half-timbered moated building was to the south-west of the present house. Only the moat survives.

St Lawrence's Church in the grounds has a Mainwaring Chapel dating from the mid-15th century and some good family monuments, including one that may date from the first decade of the 15th century. The North Chapel (of 1648) contains a handsome monument to Philip and Ellen Mainwaring. It was Ellen (*née* Minshull) who built the outstanding stables of 1654 as a present for her son, Thomas, then the squire of Peover.

As is sometimes the case, the stables (listed Grade I) are regarded as architecturally more important than the house (Grade II*). Built of brick with stone dressings and mullioned windows, the exceptionally elaborate interior features

Opposite
Peover: entrance front.

Tuscan columns and arches and an exquisite strapwork plaster ceiling.

The beneficiary of this stable block (or at least the owner of the favoured horses), Thomas Mainwaring, became Sheriff and Member of Parliament for Cheshire and was created a baronet in 1660. The adjoining pedimented coach-house (now used as a tea-room), which dates from just more than a century later, was built by his great-grandson, Sir Henry Mainwaring, 4th Baronet.

Somewhat unusually, Sir Henry succeeded to the temporarily dormant title the moment he was born in November 1726, as his uncle, the previous baronet, had died in September and his father, the only other heir, in July.

In the 1760s Sir Henry decided not only to build a new coach-house but to improve the accommodation of the old manor house itself. Already enlarged in the mid-17th century, Peover now acquired a substantial 18th-century range with a pediment. Sir Henry's designer for the work of 1764 is not known though, by way of a tentative attribution, the name of Thomas Farnolls Pritchard, the Shrewsbury architect, has been invoked.

As Sir Henry was a bachelor the baronetcy expired with him in 1797 but the estate passed to his 'uterine half-brother', Thomas Wetenhall (Miss Blackett's son by her second marriage to an Essex parson), who duly took the name of Mainwaring. The new squire's eldest son, Henry, married a Cotton from Combermere Abbey (sister of Field-Marshal 1st Viscount Combermere) in 1803 and received a new baronetcy the following year.

This Sir Henry, a celebrated local sportsman and master of the Cheshire Hunt for more than 20 years, carried out further internal improvements to the house and his grandson refaced the Georgian façade in the 1890s.

The Mainwaring baronetcy of the second creation died out in 1934; the younger daughter of the last baronet married the late Peter Cazalet, the Queen Mother's racehorse trainer. Peover had been sold, together with some 1,700 acres, in 1919 to John Peel, the son of a Manchester cotton merchant who sold the estate shortly before his death in 1940 to Harry Brooks, the Manchester furniture tycoon.

During the Second World War Peover became the headquarters of General Patton of the United States Army, whose formidable presence here is commemorated by an American flag in the church where he was a regular attender. The place was not derequisitioned from military occupation until 1950; the Brooks's restorations and alterations have been principally carried out over the last 25 years.

Randle Brooks, Harry's son who was born in 1941 and is the present squire, recalls that Peover formerly looked like an incongruous 'semi-detached': part Elizabethan and Jacobean, part Georgian. As the Georgian addition was in a particularly poor condition, the Brooks family decided to demolish the 1764 range and to concentrate on restoring the rest.

What remains is an ideally-sized, irregular structure of much charm, part two-storeyed with gables and part three-storeyed with parapets and mullion and transom windows. The demolished Georgian wing in the centre has been replaced by a sympathetic new Elizabethan-style elevation. The credit for this is shared between Mr Brooks himself and his craftsman, Mr Sidney Smith.

Mr Brooks has embellished Peover with many excellent features rescued from demolished country houses. The fine rococo iron gates come from Alderley Park, seat of that eccentric local dynasty, the Stanleys of Alderley; and some of the panelling in the morning room comes from another Cheshire seat associated with the Stanleys, Grafton Hall. The wooden pilasters installed in the dining-room were brought in from the demolished Horsley Hall in Denbighshire.

The Brooks family's biggest haul came, appropriately enough, from the seat of another branch of the Mainwaring family, Oteley in Shropshire, which was built in the Elizabethan style in the late 1820s and demolished in 1959. The bookcases in the upstairs drawing-room and the more flamboyant panelling in the morning room are of Oteley provenance. The bedrooms at Peover are noted for their collection of wooden beds.

Plenty of panelling, as in the Oak Bedroom, also survives from the Mainwarings' time at Peover and among the other notable original features is the open timber ceiling in the old sunken kitchen. This room has been fitted up as a Great Hall (complete with armour) and recently redecorated by Randle Brooks's wife, the former Juliet Aschan, a grand-daughter of the late Samuel Guinness, the merchant banker. A well-known figure in the art world, Mrs Brooks is the proprietor of Grand Tours, the cultural travel company.

Mrs Brooks is also responsible for much of the interior redecoration and for the replanting of the gardens, which are noted for their topiary. Future prospects include the implementation of the architect Rory Young's engaging plans for a new layout round the swimming-pool behind the house.

In the park, which was landscaped in the 18th century, Mr Brooks has planted a new spinney to add to the 300 acres of woods on his land. Whereas the acres of so many family seats have contracted in recent generations, those connected with Peover have increased manifold through the Brooks family's purchase of the neighbouring Tatton estate (the house being bequeathed to the National Trust) following the death of the last Lord Egerton of Tatton in 1958.

The family estate thus comprises a total of some 5,500 acres, of which 700 acres are farmed in hand (arable) and the rest let out to 30 tenant farmers. Mr Brooks runs a syndicated shoot on the estate, whose other sporting connection is as the home of the Cheshire Forest Kennels.

A knowledgeable amateur of country houses and a passionate believer in their survival as privately-owned family seats, Mr Brooks has already taken steps to secure the continuity at Peover by obtaining 'heritage' exemption from capital transfer tax. The third generation of the family are Mr and Mrs Brooks's young children, Henry and Serena. In a county celebrated for its long tenures, this new dynasty seems well set for survival.

Peover Hall, Over Peover, near Knutsford, Cheshire, is open as advertised in the summer.

CROSSMAN
OF TETWORTH

Sir Peter and Lady Crossman.

WHEN sorting out 'country houses' from houses in the country, it is not the size of the building that matters (for 'seats' encompass castles to manor houses) but whether or not the 'messuage' (the legal term) is the capital of an agricultural estate.

At first glance Tetworth Hall in Cambridgeshire, with its red brick, five-bay façade, might appear like a rectory or superior house in a village. In fact, it is set in its own park at the centre of a 3,000-acre estate owned by Sir Peter Crossman, former chairman of the National Union of the Conservative Party, of Watney Mann and of the Brewers Society. Whatever Tetworth lacks in quantity—though it is an ideal size for today—the charm of the Queen Anne architecture more than compensates in quality. Tetworth's county affiliation begs a question or two. Although now officially situated in Cambridgeshire, its postal address is Sandy, Bedfordshire, while historically it must be said to belong to the erstwhile county of Huntingdonshire. It has a connection with Huntingdon's most celebrated son, Oliver Cromwell, the Lord Protector.

After the Dissolution of the Monasteries, the lands of Wistow, which originally belonged to Ramsey Abbey, were acquired by Sir Richard Williams, a nephew of Henry VIII's henchman, Thomas Cromwell, whose surname he took. They were subsequently sold in the mid-17th century by Sir Oliver Cromwell (who, unlike his nephew and namesake was a staunch royalist) to Sir Nicholas Pedley, serjeant-at-law, from a prominent local family.

In 1705 Pedley's son, John, later MP for Huntingdonshire, extended the estate by buying the manor of Tetworth. A contemporary map in the present owner's possession shows the site where Tetworth Hall now stands to have then been occupied by the 'homestead' of one Richard Barratt. It seems possible that John Pedley's new early-18th-century

Above
Tetworth Hall, Bedfordshire:
entrance front.

structure may have incorporated part of this previous building.

John Pedley's architect is not known, but the work was of a highly satisfying calibre. The entrance front is flanked by two giant rusticated stone pilasters; the front door has a stone frame with engaged Corinthian columns supporting a pediment containing a cartouche of arms. The armorial bearings displayed are Pedley impaling Foley, in allusion to John Pedley's marriage to Miss Essex Foley.

There have been comparatively few changes to Tetworth since it was built in 1710. Later in the 18th century the glazing bars in the sash windows appear to have been altered; a curved bay was added on the west side to the drawing-room and the bedroom over it; and while some authorities state that the service wing was added to the east, Sir Peter Crossman and others believe that this wing could have been part of the old homestead.

Inside, Tetworth is blessed with largely untouched crisp, contemporary detail. There is pleasing bolection-moulded panelling in several rooms. The finest interior is the entrance hall with two Corinthian columns screening the splendid oak staircase which rises in three flights against the side walls. On the landing upstairs are two exuberantly carved doorcases featuring cherubs and foliage.

The Pedleys remained seated at Tetworth until the death of their spinster heiress in 1827, after which the estate was inherited by their cousins, the Foleys, a branch of the Herefordshire family seated at Stoke Edith. Henry Foley, son of Major-General Richard Foley, retained the Wistow part of the Pedley property—which passed to the Thorntons at the end of the 19th century—but sold Tetworth to Charles Duncombe, 1st Lord Feversham, at about the time of Queen Victoria's accession to the throne. Lord Feversham, a magnate from Yorkshire, was buying up various estates in the area in the 1830s, including Waresley Hall, the Huntingdonshire seat of the Irish Earls of Kilmorey.

For the next hundred years or so Tetworth was let out for the most part, the tenants including a branch of the Orlebars of Hinwick in Bedfordshire. In the 1930s another important Bedfordshire family, the Pyms of Hazells, bought the estate from the sporting 3rd Earl of Feversham (remembered for this curious habit of encouraging hounds with the cry 'Greta Garbo, Greta Garbo'; and also for throwing that lady's friend Cecil Beaton into the River Nadder on one notorious occasion at Wilton).

At the beginning of the Second World War, during which the house was requisitioned by the Army, Tetworth acquired yet another absentee landlord, the racing peer, the 7th Earl of Sefton. He presumably bought the place because of its proximity to Newmarket, but he never lived there.

The connection of the present owner with Tetworth goes back nearly half a century. Sir Peter first rented the house on a furnished tenancy in 1937 shortly before taking up the Mastership of the Essex and Suffolk Foxhounds. After the Second World War, in which he served with the Warwickshire Yeomanry in the Middle East and Italy, he became the tenant of Tetworth once more, and finally bought the whole estate from Lord Sefton in 1962.

The Crossmans are a well-known Devonian, Northumbrian and East Anglian brewing dynasty long associated with the equally sporting family of Mann. The Cambridgeshire Hunt has had a virtually unbroken succession of Crossman Masters this century, including Sir Peter himself; his second wife (who is also his first cousin); and both her parents.

Sir Peter was knighted in 1981 following a distinguished career in brewing and 'grassroots' Tory politics. As chairman of Huntingdon Steeplechases for 15 years he did much to put his local course on the map and, as an owner, he has had a number of jumpers in training with Harry Thomson Jones at Newmarket, notably the prolific winner Pavement Artist. His younger son, Anthony, is a former clerk of the course at Goodwood and Lingfield. Sir Peter has three children and eight grandchildren from his first marriage to Monica Barnett.

Tetworth is a sporting estate. 'We strongly believe that the country sports—hunting, shooting and fishing—should happily co-exist,' Sir Peter says. 'The land is both hunted and shot over regularly.' In the summer Sir Peter fishes the Lochy in Inverness-shire from a house shared at Fort William with a member of the Mann family. His gamekeeper, Angus Nudds, a colourful East Anglian character and author of some evocative reminiscences, is in full sympathy with Sir Peter's all-round sporting approach. A practical conservationist and former member of the Farming and Wildlife Agricultural Group, Sir Peter is a staunch advocate of the sport's role in the countryside: 'There wouldn't be half the woodlands if it weren't for shooting'.

There are about 500 acres of woodland on the Tetworth estate, some 650 acres are farmed in hand (arable) and the rest is let to four tenants. Unusually for this part of the country, the soil is suitable for rhododendrons and azaleas; they are a special feature of the woodland and pond garden at Tetworth. The position of the house on an eminence, affording glorious views at the back, is also somewhat unexpected for this traditionally 'flat' country. The terrace and balustrades were laid out by the landscape architect Vernon Daniells, in the 1950s.

The other modern architect associated with Tetworth is the late Marshall Sisson, an eminent 'neo-Georgian' whose work receives high praise in John Martin Robinson's *The Latest Country Houses*. In the early 1960s Sisson created the present library out of two rooms in the east wing and designed the loggia on the west side of the house.

The Crossmans, who open the gardens twice a year for charity, are engagingly modest about the house's claim to be a 'family seat', but there can be no question of the merits of this lovingly restored home. Tetworth is certainly a most enviable example of a Queen Anne manor house—a miniature gem.

Opposite
Tetworth Hall: hall and staircase.

Tetworth Hall, near Sandy, Bedfordshire, is not open to the public, though the gardens are open by appointment.

EPILOGUE

SINCE the preceding articles were written, Bettiscombe (probably my personal favourite among the family seats I covered) has, alas, been sold and so has Orchardleigh (now, I understand, to be a country house hotel). Lady Agnes Eyston of Hendred, Tom Blofeld of Hoveton, Sir Walter and Lady Burrell of Knepp, Colonel John Cookson of Meldon, Arthur Duckworth of Orchardleigh, Peter Montgomery of Blessingbourne and Jean Foster of Lexham have all died. And Simon Courtauld has departed from the editorial chair at *The Field*—an event which caused me to bring my 'Family Seats' series to an end.

Index

PICTURE CREDITS

Eric Crichton: Cruwys of Cruwys Morchard, Dymoke of Scrivelsby, Staunton of Staunton, Mynors of Treago, Heneage of Hainton, Houison Craufurd of Craufurdland, Munro of Foulis, Hanham of Deans Court, Graham of Norton Conyers, Milbank of Barningham, Foljambe of Osberton, Gordon Duff of Drummuir, Williams of Caerhays, Farquharson of Braemar, Godsal of Iscoyd, Hobhouse of Hadspen, Phillips of Wombourne Wodehouse, Weld of Chideock, Duckworth of Orchardleigh, Pinney of Bettiscombe, Forbes Adam of Skipwith, Crossman of Tetworth

David Davison: O'Conor of Clonalis, Lefroy of Carrigglas, Lowry of Blessingbourne

Alistair Morrison: Leighton of Loton, Eyston of Hendred, Fetherstonhaugh-Frampton of Moreton, Puxley of Welford, Jeffreys of Newhouse, Blofeld of Hoveton, Jay of Derndale, Plumptre of Goodnestone, Burrell of Knepp Castle, Cookson of Meldon, Capel Cure of Blake Hall, Foster of Lexham, Ropner of Thorp Perrow, Brooks of Peover

Glyn Satterley: Charlton of Hesleyside, Steuart Fothringham of Murthly

ACKNOWLEDGEMENTS

I WOULD like to thank all the owners of the Family Seats for their generous help in the preparation of the articles; the various photographers with whom it was almost always a pleasure to collaborate; the former editor and staff of *The Field* (particularly the chief sub-editor, Anne Wright, even if she did tread unsoftly on too many of my now forgotten jokes); my literary agent Gillon Aitken; my secretary Cynthia Lewis; and, above all, my inspiring mentors in these matters— James Lees-Milne, Mark Bence-Jones, John Martin Robinson, Peter Reid and Michael Sayer.